"I guess we have a few things in common, don't we?"

"A few," he said with a smile.

Leah felt as though a lead weight had somehow been lifted from her shoulders—one she never knew had burdened her until the words came forth. "Anyway, now you know why I can't let go of this. I always thought perhaps I should go into detective work, but I love writing. Maybe, somehow, the two can come together." She hesitated, thinking once again of Chet's accusations. "We've got to get to the crux of this thing, Jim. You know, there are people accusing you of being involved in the incident."

Jim's face blanched at the news. He nearly fell over on the bench. "What? You–you can't be serious. Who is saying this?"

"I can't say right now, Jim, but rumors are floating around."

He brushed a hand across his face. "This can't be happening. Leah. . ." His voice trailed away. "Leah, you don't think that I could have. . ."

LAURALEE BLISS, a former nurse, is a prolific writer of inspirational fiction as well as a home educator. She resides with her family near Charlottesville, Virginia, in the foothills of the Blue Ridge Mountains. Lauralee invites you to visit her web site at: http://lauraleebliss.homestead.com.

HEARTSONG PRESENTS

Books by Lauralee Bliss
HP249—Mountaintop
HP333—Behind the Mask

A Rose Among Thorns

Lauralee Bliss

Heartsong Presents

To Jennifer Ferranti, whiz of the impossible interview and a great mentor in my early writing days. With thanks to Nannie Nehring-Bliss for her artistic conception of a rose among thorns.

This book was inspired by teacher Shannon Wright, who gave her life to save her students that fateful day in Jonesboro, Arkansas, March 24, 1998.

A note from the author:

I love to hear from my readers! You may correspond with me by writing:

Lauralee Bliss
Author Relations
PO Box 719
Uhrichsville, OH 44683

ISBN 1-58660-387-6

A ROSE AMONG THORNS

Scripture taken from the HOLY BIBLE: NEW INTERNATIONAL VERSION®. NIV®. Copyright © 1973, 1978, 1984 by International Bible Society. Used by permission of Zondervan Publishing House.

Cover illustration by Lorraine Bush.

PRINTED IN THE U.S.A.

one

Jim Richards whispered thoughts of love while he knelt before the television, tracing her delicate features with a sweep of his finger. A wide forehead covered by a mass of curly bangs and a face with blushing cheeks met his gaze. Her eyes were deep set and dark brown, framed by long, thick eyelashes and eyebrows that matched the color of her hair. When she smiled, her gleaming teeth brightened her entire face. The smile drew forth a similar one on his face. She then waved at him before walking away to take a seat on the sofa and crossing her slender legs. How he loved to stare at her legs. The rose-print skirt and blush-colored blouse, typical of a teacher's outfit, outlined her trim figure.

"Hey, that's enough filming, Jim!" her voice rang out.

"Okay, but let me get it from this angle."

"Do you have to?" Despite the petulant voice, her face continued to display the award-winning smile that stirred his heart. The camera turned and zoomed in again on her facial features, carefully made up to perfection. She was the neatest, prettiest woman he had ever known. She was perfect in every respect.

Just then Taffy, the squirming Scottish terrier, jumped onto her lap and tried to lick her face. "Taffy, down!" she commanded with a girlish giggle.

Jim laughed, watching the dog cover her with kisses. Her arms encircled the dog, giving him a hug before scooting him off her lap. When the next scene began to unfold, the muscles in his neck tensed like strings on a guitar. His throat became dry. Jim stretched out a finger, poised to press the stop button on the VCR.

"So, how far along are you?" asked the cameraman.

The beautiful woman before him relaxed against the sofa and patted her stomach.

"You know. Three months for this little guy."

"And just how do you know it's a boy?"

She winked. "I know."

The feelings of joy at seeing her beloved face now disintegrated into despair. With a swift thrust of a forefinger, he ejected the tape and turned off the VCR. The familiar shroud of grief engulfed him like thunderclouds from a gathering storm. Emotion flooded his heart. Stark images rocked his brain. He would never get over this. Everyone said he would with time, but the pain of the loss was too unbearable, even after a year.

Jim walked into the kitchen. Opening the refrigerator, he perused the shelves for a drink to ease the scratchy feeling in his throat. He found little to eat or drink, typical of the last twelve months. Orange juice, a packet of cheese, some luncheon meat, and a squeeze bottle of mustard stared back at him. He thought of the many people who chastised him for eating meals of luncheon meat slapped between two crusts of bread.

"It's not healthy," rang the well-meaning voices in his brain. "You must eat better than that." Many invited him to their homes for a meal, but he couldn't bear the thought of spending time with other families. The pain kept him confined in his own home where he tried to occupy his mind by surfing the Internet or reading a book. He would never open up his tortured heart to others. Here at home he felt safe, but memories continually hounded him.

Jim grabbed for the juice and poured a glass. The huge grandfather clock in the dining room ticked methodically behind him. All was quiet but for a neighborhood dog barking.

The stillness of the surroundings was a far cry from a year

ago when people from all walks of life swarmed the place. He became smothered in humanity ranging from his sister to strangers off the street who heard the tragic news. Zillions of reporters aimed microphones and cameras at his face. He stiffened at the thought of those reporters probing into every facet of his life. The front door still displayed the crack from a book he threw at one reporter who hurried out of his home to avoid the missile. After the incident, Jim bolted his doors, took his phone off the hook, and refused all callers.

Of course his actions did not keep out his younger sister, Claire. She found a way to access his house by using the key he kept inside a plastic rock labeled *Kindness* in the garden. "I won't leave you alone like this," her voice echoed in his brain, among the many recollections he nursed that day.

He permitted Claire her well-meaning visitations until the reporters got wind of the arrangement and began following her around. Eventually everything died down. The reporters went back to other news stories. The neighbors, having filled his home with every pie and casserole imaginable, returned to their everyday lives. He was left alone to pick up the pieces of his broken life, shattered by one horrible day that would remain with him forever.

Jim sat down heavily at the kitchen nook to gulp the orange juice. The liquid relieved his parched throat but did little to remove the lump of anguish. The faint chime of the doorbell broke through the time of contemplation. Jim put the glass in the sink and strode to the living room to glance out the window. "Claire," he whispered, before answering the front door, relieved by the familiar face.

The stout woman with strawberry blond hair immediately threw her arms around him before picking up the two shopping bags resting at her feet.

"What're those?" he asked, pointing at the bags as she walked into the house. In the living room, she paused before the videocassette lying on the carpet.

"Watching home movies again?"

He shrugged and helped her carry a bag into the kitchen.

"Which one is that?"

"The one where Taffy jumps up on Kathy's lap and licks her face."

"Oh, that one." Claire moved to the kitchen where she began unpacking the fixings for a salad and packages of chicken breasts, ham, and Swiss cheese. "I'm going to make you a feast. Chicken Cordon Bleu."

"Claire, I don't really care about. . ."

"I know, but you have to eat. You can't keep doing this to yourself, Jim. You've got to shake it off and go on. Kathy would want you to."

Jim opened the refrigerator and began throwing the food carelessly on the shelves. "I don't know what she would have wanted. I never had the chance to tell her good-bye." The tension traveled through his arms to his neck where it collected inside his head. He squeezed his eyes shut to ward off the shudder of pain.

Claire came and rubbed his shoulders with her fingers. "C'mon now. You were always good at telling me what to do when we were kids. Now I'm telling you. It's time to eat and get on with your life." She slowly turned him around. "Just look at you. You're so skinny, I'll bet you fit into a size twenty-eight."

"For your information, I'm still a thirty-two

"Well, look at me." She twirled around like a ballerina. "Size eighteen and I love every bit of myself. Besides, I know you can eat way more than I can. So I'm going to cook this meal, and you're going to eat it, or rather, we're going to eat it."

"Suit yourself." He strode out to the porch where the evening paper lay. His gaze immediately fell on the front headline: *One Year After A Deadly School Shooting, A*

Community Is Still Reeling In Shock. He noted the reporter's name: Leah Hamilton. "Must be they hired a new one for the *Gazette* after last year's fiasco." He settled down on the sofa in the living room to read the article. It began as they all did, recounting the events of that dreadful June day a year ago. His hands trembled as the memories swept over him.

Children were playing peacefully on swing sets or dangling from monkey bars when a shot suddenly rang out. In only a matter of moments, the children's third-grade teacher lay on the ground with a bullet wound to the chest, fired by an unknown sniper in a tree just beyond the school playground. Twenty-six-year-old Kathy Richards died later that afternoon at the county medical center.

Jim chewed on his lower lip. He recalled in vivid detail the news clips that ran on the television, showing the stretcher that bore his bleeding wife as she was rushed to the hospital. He was away at a conference, talking up a new computer program he had invented, only to return that afternoon after receiving a frantic call from the emergency room personnel. By the time he arrived at the hospital, Kathy had already died in the operating room. He placed the paper down on his lap. The evening before her death, Kathy had diligently pressed his shirts for the conference and given her usual warning not to get them mussed up during the trip. She even packed the travel iron after instructing him on how to use it. "I want you looking your best when you give your speech," she told him. "Don't forget to polish your shoes and take your toiletry kit. And please wear your nice aftershave."

He recalled his vexation at all her orders that reminded him of a doting mother. Guilt washed over him for not thanking her, instead. That morning he whispered a quick "I love you" and deposited a careless kiss on her lips before running to his car for the long, three-hour trip. How he wished he had known the future. If there were some way he could have known, he would have spent time talking to her. . .holding her. . .whispering in her ear until she giggled. . .telling her how much he loved her. He would have forsaken the whole conference and whisked her away on a second honeymoon, away from the violence and hatred in the world. Jim dropped his head and closed his eyes. No, he had left her alone that terrible day. He had assumed it would be like any other. He thought he would be a father in less than four months. . .until everything ended in one horrific blast from a murderer's weapon.

He choked. A tear drifted down one cheek. He swiped it away with an angry flick of his finger. He rattled the paper, searching the paragraph to resume reading the article.

The police continue to follow leads in the case but have made no arrests. Cries for justice echo all around the community of Bakersville. Families have joined together to offer a reward for any information leading to the arrest and conviction of the person or persons responsible. Taylor Elementary has stepped up security, and a police officer has been on duty full time since the beginning of the school year.

"Where was this police officer a year ago?" Jim grumbled. "Why does someone have to die before they start doing what's right? It's the same thing with traffic lights. They will install them at an intersection only after someone is killed. . . like the action can bring back the dead. Well, it can't. Nothing can."

"What are you muttering about?" Claire came out of the kitchen, clad in his chef's apron with a huge lobster printed on front. Kathy gave him the apron after an excursion to Maine. Another memory flashed before his eyes—of ocean waves pounding the rocky shores, of Kathy's huge smile and dancing eyes. They'd eaten lobster, then taken an evening stroll to observe the flicker of lights from distant ports of call. More pain stabbed at him at the mere sight of the apron.

"Oh, you're reading the paper."

Jim rattled the paper to emphasize his distress. "Yeah, they got some new dame working on the news staff. She paints the killing like it's an anniversary celebration or something. Let's bake a cake and blow up balloons while we're at it." Jim dashed the section of the newspaper to the floor in frustration. "Reporters love gory stuff. They eat it up like it's candy. I'll bet they go to bed at night praying that someone gets raped, maimed, or gutted by gunfire. It makes their day and their paycheck. They live for the news while others die to make the news."

"Now, Jim—" Claire began.

"No, I mean it. And I'll bet they're glad the police haven't solved this. What would they have to report? No one really cares what's going on. Everyone has decided this thing will remain unsolved, no matter what. I hear how the trail has gone cold. The longer the police wait, the more time that animal has to run. This will never be solved. Never."

"Jim, c'mon and help me cut up the ham and Swiss cheese," Claire coaxed. "You can't keep tormenting yourself like this."

Jim ignored her request and swiped up the sports section. "I'm reading the baseball stats," he informed her before peering over the top of the page to watch her disappear into the kitchen. Immediately he regretted his selfish attitude. Claire was only trying to help. At this point in his life, Jim didn't want help. No one could help him—not the investigators, family, or his well-meaning neighbors, the Hansons. Even God had abandoned him, taking from him those most precious in his life—his wife and his unborn child. There was nothing left in this world. Perhaps he would do better to seek a final solution to the pain, but he cast the idea aside in an instant. If Claire ever caught wind of what was circulating in his brain, she would call a shrink and have him locked up. Suicide was not the answer, but what was? What could he do to change his circumstances?

two

Leah Hamilton stood before the mirror, brushing her dark brown hair with long strokes until it shone. She placed the brush on the vanity, then turned sideways, watching her hair flow down her back like ripples of chocolate taffy. Many of her coworkers jibed her about her long hair. They thought it too old-fashioned in a day of short hairstyles for the active woman. Leah shrugged and picked up bobby pins to fasten the flowing hair into a bun at her nape. Her differences did not seem to hurt her status at work.

Having just become a reporter for the *Bakersville Gazette*, Leah found herself winning the respect of her superiors in a short length of time. Before the job at the *Gazette*, Leah prided herself on obtaining difficult interviews with high-profile personalities who came through the state. She carried on in that vein when she joined the staff on the *Gazette*. After a few successful interviews with celebrities, the editor-in-chief switched her to human-interest stories. A few weeks ago, he assigned her the job of writing an anniversary update on the Taylor Elementary School shooting. Leah found the story to be heartbreaking and one of the most difficult pieces she had ever written. During her in-depth research of the facts, the news staff was quick to warn her not to call the slain teacher's husband.

"The guy's a basket case," the secretary informed Leah after helping her find some needed information. "He threw a book at our last reporter, Chet Frazier. It wasn't a paperback either, but a coffee-table variety. Chet said it was like a missile."

Leah widened her eyes in surprise. "You're kidding."

"I wish I was. I suppose I'd feel the same way if something happened to my Gary and I had reporters pestering me for details. But still, we're only trying to do our job here at the *Gazette*. People are eager to find out what's going on. They like to read these kinds of stories."

"And stories sell newspapers," Leah finished.

"That's what Mr. Sanders would say."

"You're right. That's what he would say. However, instead of plowing in there without any sense of feeling for the victim's family, we need to put ourselves in their shoes. Take this Mr. Richards, for instance. I'm sure he was grieving for his wife at the same time that reporter was hounding him for an interview. Most people want privacy during times of grief. They don't want someone sticking his nose where it isn't wanted."

"So how do you get around it?"

"You learn to empathize. You listen. You make yourself an outlet for their grief instead of hemming them in with questions. I find it easier to talk to women that way than men. We women love to discuss how we're feeling. Men keep it all bottled up until one day they explode. Maybe that was what happened to Mr. Richards when he chased Chet Frazier out of his home."

The secretary stared at Leah admiringly. "Are you married?"

"No," she said with a chuckle.

"Why do you laugh?"

"Because that's the proverbial question everybody asks me. 'Are you married?' And when I say no, then they ask if I'm seeing anyone."

"For someone not married, you sure know a lot about relationships."

"It's all analysis, pure and simple. When you write personality profiles, you learn quite a bit about people."

Leah continued to muse over the conversation concerning

this Mr. Richards as she groped for a bottle of perfume and dabbed the scent behind her ears. His obstinate nature intrigued her. The idea of someone refusing an interview set up a challenge. Her mind began devising ways to make the interviewee acquiesce.

Only if Mr. Sanders wants it, she thought. *Whatever Mr. Sanders wants, he gets. He's the boss and the one who makes everything at the paper come together*. From the reporters to the typesetters to the deliveries, Mr. Rex Sanders coordinated it. She was a mere subordinate, willing to do whatever he ordered and hoping one day to advance up the career ladder if her work warranted it.

Leah selected a crisp suit, still encased in plastic from the dry cleaners, from her wardrobe. While other reporters wore relaxed outfits of pants and blouses, Leah insisted on looking professional, even if she sat behind a desk typing up a draft on a computer notepad. Clothes were a part of her mainstay in life. Surveying the six suits staring back at her from the padded hangers, she wondered if it was time to hit a major city and check out the department stores. Another couple of suits to join those in the closet might enhance her job performance at the *Gazette*. After all, she was now a newspaper reporter. Her title required the look and confidence of one who knew the business. She slid on the skirt, tucked in an ivory silk blouse, then slipped her arms into the jacket. A pair of tan pumps from her vast shoe collection completed the outfit.

Leah strode out to the small kitchen nook where she grabbed a glass of juice before checking the time. "No time for breakfast again," she muttered. "I'd better start getting up earlier."

Traffic was a nightmare as she negotiated her sporty vehicle along the long lines of cars headed for the job world. At last she turned into the stark brick building with the *Bakersville Gazette* sign prominently displayed. She ignored various stares from people also arriving for work, including the typesetter, Richard, and the custodian named Sam Warner who never ceased to issue some lewd remark.

"Looking good this morning, Ms. Hamilton." Warner whistled, his eyes narrowing in appreciation. "How 'bout you and me grabbing some lunch later today?"

The image of his dirty clothes and grizzled face behind some counter at an all-night diner sent a shiver up her spine. Leah shook her head in disgust and pushed her way through the glass doors, nodding at the secretary who directed incoming calls to the different departments. Leah arrived at her desk and checked her voice-mail messages. "Mr. Sanders will meet with you today at nine A.M. sharp," announced the boss's secretary.

Leah tucked back a single strand of dark brown hair that had fallen out of the chignon. "Wonder what he wants?" She grabbed herself a mug of freshly brewed coffee before heading off to the boss's office, located in the opposite wing of the building. She entered and issued a professional good morning to Mr. Sanders, who sat at his desk.

"Come right in, Ms. Hamilton. Have a seat, please, and I'll be with you shortly."

Leah sat opposite his desk in the padded, high-back chair and crossed her legs. She sipped on her coffee while waiting for him to complete his work. Behind him on a table stood framed pictures of his family, including his wife, four children, and numerous relatives. Leah liked the idea of working for a family man. Despite his caustic attitude that occasionally tested her and the other members of the staff, Mr. Sanders was a man of principle. She singled out each object decorating the desk before turning her attention to a framed print hanging on the wall. Squinting, she tried to make out the phrase outlined in color on a raised surface.

"It's a Proverb from the Bible, Ms. Hamilton," he told her.

"I've never seen anything so unusual. It appears almost three dimensional."

"It's the artist's own rendition—quite imaginative, I might add." He leaned back, his eyelids drooping until his eyes were mere slits as he quoted, " 'Trust in the Lord with all your heart and lean not on your own understanding.' " His eyes popped open, and he straightened in his chair. "It's my wife's favorite verse. Unfortunately, I've had a hard time accepting it in a place like this. I try to conquer the challenges myself. Not always a wise idea."

Leah wondered what he meant by the comment. He lifted up Monday's edition of the *Gazette* from his desk. "I liked your story, Ms. Hamilton."

"Thank you, Sir."

"You possess a flair for poignant writing, which is very much needed in these human-interest stories."

"I guess it comes from the personality profiles I did before this job. I hate the straight—'I asked, I said.' I like a little extra sugar. Makes the story easier to swallow, so to speak."

Sanders nodded in approval. "That's what I've heard. You've interviewed quite a few famous people."

Leah shrugged, trying to appear modest despite the pride that filled her being. "I do the best job I can."

"Actually, I have a personality profile I would like for you to handle. It's been rather difficult to obtain in the past." He inhaled deeply. "I believe strongly that the readers would be interested in knowing more about the slain teacher's husband from the elementary school shooting."

"You mean Jim Richards?"

"Right. You may have heard that during the weeks following the death of his wife, he was a difficult man to interview. Nearly impossible, as a matter of fact."

"I've heard that was the case."

Sanders eyed her with interest. "We'd like an update a year

after the incident. You think you're capable of handling it, Ms. Hamilton?"

A tingle of excitement shot through her. "Without a doubt, Sir. It's my specialty."

A small smile formed on his face. "Good. Your assignment, then, is to get an exclusive interview with this Mr. Richards. I think if we can nail it, we're sure to capitalize on a huge selling point with the readers."

Leah set down her coffee mug on a nearby stand, fished out a small notepad from her leather satchel, and began jotting a few notes. "Anything in particular you wish for me to find out, Mr. Sanders?"

"The usual. How he's coping. What he thinks about the investigative probe into his wife's murder, or the lack thereof. If he's angry with the police."

Leah nodded.

"And what he's doing with his life right now—hobbies, love interests, that sort of thing. Anything the readers will eat up. I'm sure you know better than I what the piece should contain."

Leah nodded with confidence, ready to toss back her long hair when she realized the strands were fastened in a bun behind her head. "I have a general idea, Sir. It should be no trouble at all."

"Fine. Make whatever contacts are necessary to get the job done. You might find it helpful to do a little research ahead of time in the archives and perhaps even contact Chet Frazier. He did the work on this case a year ago. He managed to associate himself somewhat with Mr. Richards's sister and was making progress until Mr. Richards got wind of it and shut off communication."

Leah clicked her long fingernails, painted a vivid red, on the armrest of the chair. "This Mr. Richards sounds like a difficult individual. . ."

". . .who requires the expertise of a skilled reporter." Sanders rose from his seat and extended his hand. "I look forward to hearing your results, Ms. Hamilton."

"Thank you, Sir," she said, pumping the hand he offered. Outside the door, Leah blew out a sigh, preparing herself for a tough race ahead. Her heels clicked along the hallway as she headed for the archives. Once inside, she pored over articles about the incident, trying to glean any new information about the slain teacher, Kathy Richards.

"She taught third grade," Leah mused. "She was loved by the students, parents, and fellow teachers. She served on the PTO and organized a school-wide craft sale every year to raise money." Her eyes then fell on something she missed the first go-around. "Kathy was five months pregnant the day of her death." That fact stabbed Leah deep in her heart. Few people ever came close to the wall Leah maintained while interviewing personalities. The facts surrounding this tragedy could not help but jump over the wall, right into her heart. "Not only did Jim Richards lose a wife, but a child too. Did he have other children, I wonder?" A quick scan of the material showed no living children. Leah sat back and sighed. "This is so pitiful. What a terrible thing to have happen."

She tried to imagine that day a year ago in the schoolyard—the cheerful sounds of the children playing, beautiful Kathy reprimanding a few of the children who ran too fast, and then the sound of gunfire. Leah closed her eyes when she saw the young woman fall to the ground, her hands covering her womb and the tiny infant who would never see the light of day.

"Oh, God," Leah whispered softly, "why did You let this happen to an innocent woman and a little baby? Why is it the innocent ones are always killed? Don't You care?" She sat, stunned by the pain of the event. *How can I possibly interview someone like Jim Richards, who's gone through this kind of tragedy?* Interviewing highly paid personalities familiar with the limelight was one thing; decorating the front of the *Gazette* with the agony of Jim Richards was something entirely different.

Leah sat still, puzzled over how to proceed. Mr. Sanders had placed his confidence in her. If she failed to obtain the interview, all her hopes and dreams of rising in the ranks, perhaps even landing a prestigious position on a national paper like *USA TODAY,* would go up in smoke. There would be nothing to show for her years of writing. "I can't let this get to me," she said with resolve. "I have to forget the emotion, forget the pain in all this, and just do my job."

Leah walked back to her office. On the laptop, she typed out an outline to help her organize the interview. A check of her supplies inside a leather satchel revealed the tiny tape player used to record the interviews. Most people loved to hear their voices on a recorder. She wondered if Richards would be the same. "More than likely, he'll throw the recorder in my face," she murmured, recalling how Chet Frazier ducked the book tossed in his direction. In light of that, Leah thumbed through a Rolodex to retrieve the number of the *Gainsport Herald,* Frazier's new employer. "Chet Frazier, please," she said to the secretary and waited.

"*Gainsport Herald*, Chester A. Frazier speaking."

"Mr. Frazier, this is Leah Hamilton from the *Bakersville Gazette.*"

"Ah yes, my replacement, if I'm not mistaken." Leah heard the rattle of papers over the receiver. "I was just reading the paper from earlier in the week. So you were blessed with the anniversary story on the elementary school shooting. Interesting writing."

"That's why I'm calling. Mr. Sanders would like an exclusive interview with Mr. Richards—an update, a year after the incident."

"You're wasting your time."

"I know you think so, but. . ."

"I know so."

Leah shrugged off the comment. "Anyway, I was wondering if you could fill me in on what happened so I might have some idea of what to expect. Better to go prepared than be surprised."

A sigh escaped through the receiver. "You want the short or the long of it?"

"Whatever gets me the most information."

"Smart woman. All right, meet me at the deli on Main Street for lunch, and I'll fill you in."

Leah wrote down the information.

"And although this is a business luncheon, let's also call it a blind date."

"Now, Mr. Frazier, I—" she began, sensing warmth fill her neck.

"The name's Chet, and I insist. If you want the inside scoop, you have to play by my rules."

"All right, just this once. I don't intend to make a habit of this."

"We'll see. Noon, then." The phone clicked in her ear. Leah replaced the receiver with a shaky hand, rattled by the manipulation of the man who had suddenly turned a business interview into a date. *The nerve of that guy. I should expect as much. He's a reporter, just like me. I suppose if he wants it his way, fine, but I will get my information.*

Just before noon, Leah paused in the employee rest room to touch up her lipstick and rearrange her hairstyle. She thought of loosening the pins and allowing her mane of dark hair to fall around her shoulders, but chose instead to wind it tight at her nape, fastening it in place with a clip. After checking her outfit, Leah headed for the elevator, only to find herself riding down to the lobby with Sam Warner. A mop and bucket containing dirty water rested at his feet.

"Howdy, Ms. Hamilton," he said in a thick, Southern drawl.

Leah pushed the button, trying to ignore the leering eyes that scanned her from the top of her head to the tips of her shoes.

"Goin' somewheres?"

"A luncheon date, if you don't mind," she told him primly. The doors whisked open.

"Next time, think of little ol' me, will ya?" he answered with a laugh as she walked out of the building.

Already Leah felt the surmounting stresses of the day send a spasm running up her back. Once in the driver's seat, she popped open a tiny vial from her purse and swallowed some aspirin with the stale water left in a bottle inside the car. "The way this day is going, I'm going to need every pill," she mumbled before hitting the accelerator and proceeding on to Main Street.

Inside the deli, she scanned the customers, many in business attire, eating sandwiches and discussing the events in their lives. In the corner of the restaurant, she noticed a rather tall man with dark, wavy hair, scanning the front page of the *Gazette*. All at once, his face peered over the paper. A large hand waved her to the table.

"Ms. Hamilton, I presume?" he inquired, rising to a height of six feet.

Leah felt like a miniature figurine by comparison. She was thankful she wore her highest heels to offset her petite stature. "Mr. Frazier?"

"Chet, Sweetheart." His smile was warm, but something that Leah couldn't identify lay hidden behind his dark brown eyes. She took a seat opposite him.

"I had no idea my replacement at the *Gazette* would be so attractive," he mused, scanning every part of her face.

Leah dismissed the compliment. She took out a black notepad, a pen, and her trusty tape recorder.

"Can't the interrogation wait until after we've had something to eat?"

Leah shrugged. He pushed a menu in her direction. She fixed her gaze on the selections, avoiding his penetrating look that left her feeling exposed. When the waitress arrived, she ordered a chef salad with light dressing and iced tea.

"I'll have corned beef on rye," Chet told the waitress. "Pile it on thick with melted Swiss cheese and lots of sauerkraut."

Leah gulped, wondering if she would have the stomach to interview the man after witnessing such a lunch. When she glanced up, Chet was staring at her with an amused expression written on his face.

"You're turning green. Not fond of my selection?"

"Let's just say I've heard better." When the beverages arrived, Leah drank her iced tea to lubricate the dryness in her throat.

"So, what did you do before the *Gazette?*" Chet wondered.

"Personality profiles for major magazines."

He raised a dark eyebrow. "Why did you switch to newspaper reporting?"

"I'm hoping to broaden my experience so I can land another job, preferably with *USA TODAY.*"

Chet nodded. "You land this interview with Richards, and I daresay you're halfway there. I wish you all the luck in the world. You're going to need it."

"I'm sure Jim Richards is not the monster everyone's painted him to be. I mean, a year has passed since his wife's death."

"Think again." His sandwich arrived, dripping with sauerkraut juice and melted cheese. Leah averted her gaze to her salad, trying to ignore him while he dug into the sandwich with all the gusto of a hungry animal. She stabbed at a cherry tomato with her fork and placed it in her mouth. They said little as they ate their lunch. When Chet finished the sandwich, he sat back in contentment.

"That hit the spot. Now I'm ready for my interview."

Leah pushed her remaining salad aside and checked the tape recorder. "Is it all right if I tape our conversation?"

"Go right ahead."

"So, tell me about your efforts to interview Mr. Richards."

Chet leaned forward, his face a bit too close for comfort, and clasped his hands together.

Leah responded by sliding her chair back a few inches.

"He's one nasty character with a mean streak that runs deeper than in anyone I've ever met. I'm the kind of guy who believes in leaving someone alone in their misery. . .but up until a point. After a week or two, I think it's time for a public statement. Did Mr. Richards give me one? Absolutely not. Even after weeks went by, he said I was invading his privacy. He called me names that I dare not repeat to a woman and even threw a book at me that damaged the front door. Not a pretty sight. I should have charged him with attempted assault."

Leah clicked off the tape player. "Really, Chet, charging a poor man with assault after he just lost his wife?"

The cheerful expression on the reporter's face disintegrated into indignation. "The guy's a basket case. He needs professional help. I tell you, with his kind of aggression, it's a wonder he isn't a suspect in his wife's death."

Leah gasped at the mere suggestion. "Chet!"

"I'm serious." He stirred in his seat. "Look, Leah, you can tell I'm a nice guy. Have you heard me raise my voice since we began this little interview? Of course not. I take things calm and cool. I try to make the other person like me so I can get the scoop too, just like all talented reporters."

"Not by ordering the kind of sandwich you did. Ugh."

He chuckled. "Okay, so I let my appetite get in the way of learning all about the attractive woman sitting before me. Next time I won't be so self-centered. Anyway, I gave this Richards a chance. I was nice and polite. I called. I rang the doorbell. I tried to get his sister to talk. I even thought of sending him boxed chocolates or a three-foot sub."

"I guess he felt you were pushing him too much."

"Maybe, but I figured he would get over it with time. Most people do. You go through the mourning stage, then it's time to speak. There's nothing like spilling your guts to the media. I thought he would be like everyone else—eager to get out the anger and the frustration in an interview, and not," he paused, "by trying to assault me."

Leah frowned. "So I guess you have no pointers on how to obtain an interview with this man."

"Leah, I'll be honest with you. If he hasn't cooled down by now, he won't. And if that's the case, I'd tell Mr. Sanders you'd rather keep your life than deal with the likes of that man."

three

Leah was not at all encouraged when she left the deli under a bright noonday sun. Her feet shuffled along the sidewalk to the car. She opened the door methodically, her mind fixed on the obstacles that lay before her. Many times she had confronted obstinate people reluctant to share their views, but never did she encounter any of the hostility that Chet Frazier so vividly described during their luncheon. The mere thought of confronting Jim Richards with a book raised in his hand formed a lump of fear inside her stomach.

"What should I do?" she wondered aloud, leaning her head against the driver's seat. "Should I call first and introduce myself? I doubt that would work. He'd probably hang up on me before I could even say hello. Maybe I should pose as a saleslady, willing to clean his carpet for free." She slammed a hand against the steering wheel. "Whatever I do, I must confront this man. Mr. Sanders, my job, my life depends on it. I won't go by what Chet says. A year has passed. Surely Jim Richards will want to talk if I approach him in a positive, but understanding, manner."

Nodding her head at her game plan, Leah stopped by her office to pick up a folder of news clippings before proceeding through the city streets of Bakersville to the suburbs where Jim Richards lived. Along the way, she inserted a soothing classical CD into the car stereo to rid herself of the tension that turned the knotted muscles of her neck into a pain-filled lump inside her brain. If she developed a headache, nothing would be accomplished. She turned the volume up, listening to the music that filtered through the speakers. The wind brushed the trees, slowly shaking them from side to side. Pretty flower gardens framed the houses on the street where Jim Richards lived. The neighborhood was definitely upscale. From her research, she knew Jim was a computer salesman. He must make a decent income in a rapidly rising market.

At last she arrived at 233 Elderberry Lane. Leah pulled to the curb opposite the home and studied it for a time. The front gardens were filled with choking weeds that once held a variety of blooming plants. The lawn needed mowing. A country porch along the front of the home stood devoid of chairs or a porch swing. Leah opened her purse and took out a tiny pair of binoculars. The first-floor window treatments were fashioned of Grecian lace. On the second level she found the blinds tightly closed, as if to block any images of the world outside. The house was in desperate need of professional cleaning, with black mold infiltrating the blue siding and trim, giving the place a soiled appearance.

Lowering the binoculars, Leah couldn't help the sorrow that welled up within her. The home spoke of a man caught in the throes of a deep depression. "It may be useless to try and talk to him," she said to herself, "but I have to try." She grabbed her satchel and headed for the front door. The doorbell chimed, but no one answered. Glancing around to make certain no one was watching, Leah slipped around the side of the home and peered into the window of an empty garage. "He's gone all right. There goes Plan A."

Leah inspected the backyard, filled with foot-high grass also in desperate need of a trim. Weeds had overtaken a little garden patch in the rear of the yard. She wondered if Kathy enjoyed growing fresh vegetables. A wooden deck lined the rear of the home, devoid of patio furnishings but for a gas barbecue. To her surprise, she noticed the glass patio doors unobstructed by curtains or blinds. *Plan B.*

Gathering up her courage, Leah walked up the deck steps, cupped her hands around her eyes, and glanced through the glass to the interior of the home. The house appeared neat and orderly. No smashed dishes or objects strewn about to indicate a madman living there. She even saw a vacuum cleaner propped up against the wall. A magnificent grandfather clock, constructed of cherry, stood in one corner of a dining room. A painting hung on the wall. A glass hutch against the far wall contained fine china and crystal. "Maybe their wedding china," Leah mused. "I wonder what pattern Kathy liked?" Leah once examined patterns in an expensive department store where she pretended to pick out her favorite china, silver, and crystal. She took out her binoculars and focused them on the hutch. "It sure looks like the pattern I picked—bone white, circled by tea roses. Isn't that something?"

"What do you think you're doing, Lady?"

Leah whirled on one heel, nearly losing her balance. A strange man ascended the deck stairs, wearing dark sunglasses that hid his eyes. She felt her heart beat furiously until the man removed the glasses.

"Surprise!" Chet Frazier smiled.

Leah gasped. "Are you crazy? You scared me half to death! What are you doing here?"

"I might ask you the same thing. You enjoy snooping around as part of the interviewing process?"

"I was. . .I was making some mental pictures," she stammered, slipping her binoculars back into her satchel.

"Mental pictures of china and glassware?"

Chet's keen observation sent heat flooding her cheeks. "That's none of your business. Why are you following me around?"

"I was concerned about you coming here by yourself. I figured if there was any chance you might get clobbered by the man of the house, then I should be chivalrous and take the beating for you."

Leah tossed the strap of the satchel over her shoulder. "As you can see, he's not home."

"No, he isn't. Do you still plan on going through with this?"

"I have to. It's my job."

Chet sighed before sinking his hands into the pockets of his expensive, pleated trousers. "Okay, but I think I'll stick around, just in case."

"I wish you would leave. This is my story, and I plan to cover it."

"Never fear, I won't steal your story. I just don't want you to get hurt."

"I can take care of myself, Mr. Frazier."

All at once, the sound of a car engine entering the driveway terminated their conversation. A chill raced through Leah. She scrambled past Chet for the stairs.

"Come with me," Chet whispered, showing her a place underneath the deck. "Scoot inside."

"Are you crazy?" she whispered but followed his lanky form beneath the deck and into the tiny hideout.

"If you're going to be investigative, you might as well do it the right way."

"If he sees me, I'll never get that interview."

"Quiet. You might learn something important."

Leah strained to hear the sounds originating from within the house. Chet's stout form pressing against her, combined with the spicy scent of his aftershave, made it nearly impossible to concentrate. Through the cracks of the deck boards, she saw a sparkle of sunshine on glass and heard a swish as the glass doors parted. The wooden planks creaked under the footsteps. Leah tensed like strings on a violin. Her heart pounded audibly in her ears. She folded her arms, trying to control the tremors that seized her extremities.

Suddenly she felt hands reaching for her in the darkness of the hideout. Chet placed a finger on her lips and encircled her shaking form with the other arm. She struggled out of his grasp and shoved him away. Chet fell backward and hit the lattice siding with an audible crack.

The footsteps above pattered across the deck floor and headed down the stairs.

Now you've done it! Leah thought, staring in anger at Chet.

You pushed me! read his scowl.

The two remained silent as the man walked back and forth with his back to them, scanning the backyard. Finally, he returned to the house and slid the glass doors shut.

Leah exhaled a troubled sigh. Her hand flicked away the sweat that collected across her forehead.

"That was close," Chet whispered.

"You had no business touching me!" Leah crawled out from beneath the deck.

"You were getting pretty jittery in there, Sweetheart. I was afraid you were going to jump out and expose us. I was just trying to calm you."

"Why don't you admit it? You just couldn't wait to get me under the deck so you could put your hands on me."

"I'd be lying if I didn't say you looked pretty good in the dark, but I was trying to calm that nervous head of yours. Nothing else. Scout's honor."

Leah hissed before taking a moment to rearrange her disheveled suit. Smears of red dirt formed ugly patterns on the skirt. "There goes my hundred-dollar suit," she moaned, heading around the side of the garage and out to the street.

Footsteps trailed her to the car. "So now you're angry with me."

"You bet I'm angry. You've ruined my interview and my clothes by showing up here. You're conceited, and you're nosy. From now on, keep to your own affairs, Mr. Frazier."

Leah opened the car door and shut it in his face.

Chet raised his arms in defeat before sauntering off to his own vehicle. Leah watched him go with a frown before glancing back to the blue house belonging to Jim Richards. At that moment, a man opened the front door to the home. From his stiff posture and the tight lines running across his face, she sensed his anger at all the commotion. "What if he sees me?" Leah wondered aloud. She stayed within the safety of her vehicle, pretending to rifle through her purse in search of some object. When Jim Richards finally retreated into the house, she turned the key in the ignition and sped off. "That was a wonderful start to my interviewing process," she grumbled. "I should have never involved Chet Frazier in this whole mess."

❧

Leah tried to soothe away her anxiety that night by taking a long, relaxing bubble bath. The frothy foam and lavender-fragranced water did little to resolve the thoughts spinning around in her head. What began as a day of confidence had quickly become one of fear and uncertainty, not to mention confusion over Chester A. Frazier. Leah traced a finger through the bubbles, wondering how she could restore order to a job that appeared on the brink of failure. After mulling over the situation, she dried off, put on her favorite pair of silk pajamas, and curled up on the sofa to read through the news clippings detailing the events of the shooting. Somehow, she had to push aside the extraneous thoughts of the day and return to her duties.

For several hours, she read through the many stories, trying to get a feel for Jim Richards. By all accounts, he was a successful computer salesman who designed programs for the manufacturers. Leah noted this on her pad, along with the word—*intelligent*. He had grown up all his life in Bakersville and met Kathy while in college. They were engaged two years in order for him to rearrange his finances before they married. With this information she added in parentheses—*knows how to manage money*.

Leah recalled the pretty blue house and country porch. The Richardses could obviously afford a nice home. Before Kathy's death, they kept it neat and stylish with outdoor gardens and fine interior decorating. At that moment, she wondered what it would be like to own a home and tend her own garden. Visions of kneeling on a pad in the great outdoors, sifting through the cool earth with her fingers before tucking a little plant in the soil, made her smile. Leah shook her head and returned to the clippings. "Fat chance I would ever be caught gardening," she murmured. "I have enough to do, trying to get this interview."

A scan of the papers noted several close friends of the Richardses, including the next-door neighbors named Hanson. Leah thought for a moment before reaching underneath the coffee table for a phone book. "Hanson," she murmured, scanning the twelve Hansons listed until she came to the one living on 231 Elderberry Lane. "Time for Plan C."

"Hello, is this Mrs. Hanson? Mrs. Hanson, my name is Leah Hamilton. I'm a reporter for the *Bakersville Gazette*. I was wondering if you might—" The phone went dead. Leah pressed the redial button. "Hello? Hello?" In frustration, she punched in the number again, only to be answered with a busy signal.

"Wonderful." She tossed the phone on the couch beside her. "I don't believe this is happening."

The phone suddenly shrilled. In her haste to pick it up, the papers on her lap flew into the air and came to rest on various places across the carpet. *What else?* she moaned before answering the call. She hoped it might be Trish or one of her other friends. She needed someone to talk to. "Hello?"

"Good evening, Madam," came a deep voice, not unlike a

gentleman in fine evening attire, complete with a bow tie.

"Excuse me, but who's this?"

"Good evening, Madam," the voice repeated, accompanied by a faint chuckle.

"Look, you got the wrong number, Bud." She clicked off the phone in a hurry before stooping to gather up the papers into the file folder. Moments later, the phone shrilled once more. "If this is a prank call, I'm getting it traced," she mumbled. "Yes?"

"Don't tell me you're still uptight," came the same voice.

"Look, whoever you are. . ."

"Leah, it's Chet. What's the matter? Are you so flustered by this afternoon that you can't take a joke?"

"Chet, you're driving me up the wall."

"Am I really?"

Leah shifted the phone to her other ear. "No. I'm just frustrated. I tried calling the neighbor who lives next door to Jim Richards, and just as I started speaking, the phone went dead."

"They hung up on you," he stated matter-of-factly. "Anyone associated with the *Gazette* is enemy number one on that street. If you had asked me about contacts, I would've warned you about phones slamming in your ear or lines going dead."

Leah began picking lint off a knit afghan decorating the sofa. "So, now I'm supposed to clear all my contacts through you?"

"I could've saved you time and agony, Sweetheart. I tried every home on the block, looking for information. Most people told me to mind my own business. The Hansons are an elderly couple who thought of the Richardses like family. Mrs. Hanson taught Kathy all about gardening, and Mr. Hanson lent Jim many of his tools. They were no help to me at all. They told me quite frankly that I should leave Richards alone."

"For not having many contacts on the street, you sure know a lot."

"Persistence pays off, Sweetheart. I happen to be very

persistent in whatever I set my mind to."

Leah immediately disliked the characterization, for she had witnessed his resolve firsthand. "Anyway, what else did your persistence reward you with?"

"Kathy used to tutor for a family down the street—the Fitzgeralds. They have a little girl who is a slow learner. The little girl absolutely adored her. She called Kathy her mommy. Of course when Kathy died, the little girl was devastated. In fact, she required counseling."

"Seems to me the Richardses got along with everyone."

"They were friendly with the neighbors and associates. The teachers and parents praised Kathy to the highest. Jim has won numerous awards and approvals for his computer programs. They had it all, I guess you could say."

"Until the shooting. Tell me, do the police have any leads?"

"They have some evidence. The police sent dog teams to scan the woods. Nothing. Seems the dude vanished without a trace. He's probably hiding out on some island in the Pacific by now."

Leah shook her head as her fingers gripped the phone. "I just don't understand who would do something like this—and at an elementary school, of all places. I mean, there have been plenty of school shootings by deranged kids in the last few years. Usually they catch the kid the same day."

"As far as I know, they've extensively interviewed anyone who might have held a grudge against the school. . .all the troublemakers in the elementary, middle, and high schools. Still no solid leads."

"And it's been a year. What a tragedy. I can't imagine what Jim has gone through the last year."

"Richards had a tough break. There are many who would like to know how he copes. I think he could offer valuable lessons to society, that is, if you can ever land that interview."

"I've been trying to do just that, Mr. Frazier. For some reason, I keep running into brick walls, and one of them is you. Now I believe I asked you earlier to bug off and leave me alone."

"I heard your request, Leah; but like I said, I'm a persistent guy. I think you and I are right for each other. We make a good team. What do you say we go about this together? We can be the dynamic duo out to catch the bad guys. I'll be Batman, and you can be Catwoman."

Leah couldn't believe his audacity. Her heart thumped nervously. "No, thank you. Besides, you and I work for different papers."

"Okay, just thought I'd give it a try. But I intend to stay in contact with you. I'm curious to see where your trail leads and where it ends. Now if you ever want to call, my number here is. . ."

"Don't worry, I won't." Leah hung up before another absurd comment came out of his mouth. "I don't believe that man. I can understand why Jim Richards threw a book at him. He doesn't know when to quit!" Yet the information he provided set her thoughts into motion. Again she reached for the phone book and looked up the name of Fitzgerald. "Here goes nothing. Please, may Plan D work."

"Hello, Mrs. Fitzgerald? Hi, I used to be a friend of Kathy Richards from high school. I heard something happened to her, and I was wondering if you could help me?"

An hour later, Leah smiled at the notes she had scribbled on paper outlining a few facts about Jim Richards. Normally she would never stoop to an impersonation, but she had grown desperate for any kind of information to present to the boss. "Now I definitely have a lead in the area." She sat back with her feet crossed and arms folded. *I wonder if a similar ruse might work with Jim Richards? I have nothing to lose at this stage of the game. If I can come up with the tidbits old Chet failed to secure, then maybe he'll get off my back, and I'll be on my way to a new position with a national paper.*

Leah went to bed that night, confident of her game plan.

four

Jim wandered around the dark house in the middle of the night, plagued by the strange noises he heard earlier that day. When Kathy first died, he spent many sleepless nights nursing memories of the one stolen from him at a tender age. Now other things appeared to be at work. He called the neighbors to ask if they had seen anything suspicious around his property. Mrs. Hanson informed him in her gentle, motherly voice that she had seen nothing, though she had taken an afternoon nap. Later that evening, she phoned to tell him that a strange woman from the *Gazette* had called, seeking information about him.

"She called herself Lee. . .Lee Hampton or something," Mrs. Hanson said. "Of course, I wouldn't tell her anything. I know how much reporters have bothered you in the past."

"I'll bet it was the same one who wrote the article earlier this week," Jim said to himself. "Here come the vultures, and they won't give up until I'm picked clean." He paced the carpet, with the grandfather clock ticking in cadence with his agitation. No doubt the reporter probably wanted to know if he had seen a shrink recently, or what his blood pressure read the last time he went to the doctor.

"Nosy troublemakers, that's what they are," Jim muttered, striding to the kitchen to make himself a cup of instant coffee. Normally he detested instant coffee, but he found himself too lazy over the last year to drag out the coffeemaker and make himself a decent cup. Kathy was always good at fixing the morning coffee. During breakfast he would steal a cup while his shirttail flopped in the breeze and his tie hung loose around his neck. Kathy would tell him to settle down while she lovingly arranged the tie around his neck.

Emotion began clogging his throat. "Don't do this to yourself," Jim moaned aloud. He glanced around the empty home, filled with the memories of Kathy: wedding china sparkling in the glass hutch, the grandfather clock they picked out at an antique store, a tiny ceramic dog that looked like Taffy sitting on the whatnot shelf. He gulped. Poor Taffy. The dog couldn't take her death either. Jim walked out into the backyard one day to find Taffy lying still and cold in the middle of the overgrown garden. The vet said it was heartworm. Jim knew otherwise. Taffy had suffered a broken heart. . .just like him.

He swallowed the coffee while gazing around the house. He often considered selling the place and moving on to a different life, but what other life was there? At least here he had the support of his sister and friends. In a strange location where no one would know him, he would be far more isolated than he already was. Besides the fact that he liked the house very much. This was the place where Kathy and he had made a home after their marriage. When he looked at their belongings, it made him feel as if Kathy were still alive somehow, ready to pop her pretty head in the door at any moment.

Jim flicked off the lights and stumbled to the couch where he collapsed. He awoke many hours later to sunlight streaming through the lace curtains of the living room windows. He shook his head and stared at the clock. "Nine A.M.," he read, collapsing once more on the couch. "I'm taking the day off. I deserve it."

After a few minutes, he shuffled to the bathroom, pausing to look at his reflection in the mirror. Day-old beard stubble and dark circles beneath his hazel eyes greeted him. Kathy once told him he was the most attractive man she had ever laid eyes on. Now he looked like a truck had run over him. He turned on the faucet and threw cold water on his face. It was a morning like all the others he had endured for 365 days—a morning laced with grogginess and unending grief.

The telephone rang. Jim shuffled out to the living room, his eyelids drooping in exhaustion, and picked up the phone. "Hello?"

"Mr. Richards?"

"Yes?"

"Hi, my name is Sally Johnson. You probably don't know me, but I was a good friend of your wife's when we were in high school."

The introduction piqued Jim's curiosity. Suddenly he found himself awake and alert.

"I heard about Kathy," she went on. "I'm so sorry."

"Thanks."

"Look, I know this may sound odd, but I was wondering if I could come over and talk about what happened. Kathy and I were such good friends."

"I don't know. . . ," he began as a yawn broke across his face. "I'm still tired."

"I'm sure you are. What a terrible thing to go through. Kathy and I were the best of friends. She was such a giving person, you know. She used to help tutor the younger students in school. I always admired her very much."

Jim coughed out the phlegm that plugged his throat. "Ahem. . .well, yes, I know she was. I suppose you could come over for a few minutes."

"How about in an hour?"

"Make it two. I'm still waking up."

"Eleven o'clock then. Thank you so much, Mr. Richards. I really appreciate this."

Jim hung up the receiver and stumbled back into the master bedroom to grab a shower. The spray of cold water on his face did little to rouse him. He wondered if it was wise to have some strange friend of Kathy's bop in at a time when he found himself wrestling with the anniversary of her death. He shrugged as he vigorously wiped his face with a thick bath towel. Maybe it would do him good to share laughter over Kathy's past. Maybe the stories of her life would help ease the sorrow of her death.

Promptly at eleven, the doorbell rang. Jim checked out the window to see a woman dressed in a business suit. Dark brown hair showered across her shoulders. *She looks like a reporter,* he thought. When he cracked open the door, the woman gave him a bright smile.

"Hi, Mr. Richards. I'm Sally Johnson."

"You sure you're not a reporter?"

The woman stepped back. She adjusted the purse strap over one shoulder. "I said on the phone that I'm a friend, remember?"

Jim reluctantly stepped aside and allowed her in. He perused his guest with a wary eye, thankful Claire had come by two days ago to vacuum the carpets. Kathy often joked that he couldn't find dirt even if it was staring him straight in the face. The woman before him appeared made up to perfection, like one used to clean and pleasant surroundings. He could imagine why Kathy and she would have been friends. Kathy and a clean house went together.

"Coffee?" he inquired.

"Yes, thank you." Sally took a seat on the couch and began fiddling with something inside her purse. Jim turned and strode out to the kitchen.

"I only make instant," he called. "I hope that will do."

"That's fine, Mr. Richards."

Moments later, he returned with a steaming mug of coffee decorated with little gingerbread boys on a background of pink. "That's a cute mug," Sally observed.

"Kathy's class gave it to her for Christmas," Jim said in a soft voice. "They also gave her a T-shirt that said, 'You're the tops, Teacher.' All the kids' parents got together and collected money."

"Isn't that nice. Well, like I said on the phone, Kathy was

one in a million. I hadn't realized she'd gotten married and moved to this fabulous house." Sally's gaze darted around the living room. "It's very nice."

"We both were working, so we could afford it."

Sally placed her mug on a nearby table and asked about the situation.

"I don't like to talk about it," Jim said. "Let's just say she went to school one day and never came home."

"I did read a news article about it."

"Reporters don't tell you anything," he said stiffly. "Those nosy troublemakers are only looking for debris to elevate themselves in the eyes of those gullible enough to believe their trash. They care nothing about the pain that goes on inside the ones who suffer."

Sally shifted restlessly on the couch. She picked up her coffee, burying her face behind the picture of the gingerbread boys painted on the ceramic surface.

He went on. "Now I know what it's like for those who suffer the loss of loved ones in accidents, plane crashes, disasters, whatever. I can sympathize with them. It takes time to grieve, but the whole process is interrupted by these nosy reporters." He sighed. "Enough about that. You said you were a close friend of Kathy's?"

"Oh, we were the best of buddies in many of the classes. We used to sneak notes across the aisle to each other when the teacher wasn't looking."

A small smile creased Jim's face. "That sounds like Kathy. She was always slipping notes into my lunches. I never appreciated them until now." He bent his head. "I really took her for granted, Sally. All the little things she did for me. . .well, you know. I think about them all the time now. She kept the greatest house and always had flowers outside, waiting for me. She called them my roses in the ground. I always thought the guy was supposed to give the flowers. Kathy said that men should have flowers too." He swallowed hard. "Now

I sit by her grave with a potted plant next to me. It seems so empty. But I thank her for what she did, anyway."

A muscle twitched in Sally's smooth cheek. "And I'm sure she hears you from heaven," she said softly.

"I know she does. She was a good Christian woman. She knew how to care for the orphans and the widows. Hmm. . ." He chuckled uneasily. "Now I'm a widower. Strange how life makes a U-turn when you least expect it."

"So Kathy was your one and only?"

"Always. When I first laid eyes on her in college, I said to myself, 'That's the girl for me.' We met in class one day. . . some kind of English class with a professor who spoke with a foreign accent. She had a hard time understanding the lectures, so I helped her out. Six months later, we knew we would get married. I wanted to wait until I was financially secure before we hit the altar. You see, we both wanted kids right away. I had to make sure I could provide for them and not obligate Kathy to work after they were born." His voice trailed off when his head slumped to his chest. "I–I never saw them born. Kathy. . .she died carrying our first. I don't even know if the baby was a boy or a girl."

Sally sat still and silent, slowly turning the mug in a circle.

"I lost two that day. And still the police don't know who did it. Can you believe it? Twelve months have gone by, and nothing."

"That's awful," Sally whispered. Her face took on a faraway look, as if in another world.

Jim watched her reaction in confusion. "Look, I'm sorry I'm dumping all this on you. You're looking a little uncomfortable."

"I was just remembering an incident in my own life," she said softly. "I know a little about injustice. I had a family member drown. My little sister. . .in a pool."

Jim shuddered. "That's terrible."

"It was. I. . ." A click suddenly sounded from inside her

purse. Sally hurriedly opened her purse and laughed. "Oh, this cell phone of mine keeps making the strangest noises. Anyway, it was terrible. So I do understand a little, Jim, I mean, Mr. Richards. So the police still have no suspects in your wife's murder?"

"They're inept. They don't care. They give me reports on their leads, only to come up dry. How a murderer can kill a teacher, then walk away. . .well, I can't even say, it burns me so." Jim suddenly came to his feet. "Hey, I have an idea. Kathy's got her old senior high yearbook on a bookshelf in the basement. Maybe we can go through it, and you can show me some things you all used to do."

A look of panic crossed Sally's face. "Well, uh. . .actually, I need to leave. I took a break from work, and if I don't get back, the boss will have my neck."

"Sure, I understand. Maybe some other time."

Sally rose to her feet and smiled. "Yes, I would like that. Thanks for sharing your heart, Mr. Richards. It makes it a little easier to understand what's happened. And thanks for the coffee."

"Sure. Bye."

"Bye."

He watched her descend the porch steps and head over to a golden sports car. For some reason, the sadness that occupied his thoughts earlier that day had greatly diminished after the conversation.

❧

Back inside her car, Leah checked the tape player hidden inside her purse. "You almost gave me away, you little stinker," she said to the voice recorder. "But I have it all on tape. I'll have to make the most of it and hope that Mr. Sanders approves."

❧

Several evenings later, Jim marched wearily to the house after a hard day's work to find the evening paper waiting for him on the doorstep. He threw his sales cases on the floor, plopped down in the recliner, and perused the front page. His heart nearly ceased to beat when he saw the headline and sidebar. *Slain Teacher's Husband Speaks Out. After a year of silence, Jim Richards speaks candidly about his experiences in the aftermath of his wife's death.*

"How can this be?" Jim cried. "I didn't speak to anyone." He noted the reporter's name. *Leah Hamilton.*

Rage filled him. "That was no Sally Johnson who came here the other day, asking me all those questions. It was that Hamilton woman." Jim threw the paper on the floor and stalked over to the telephone.

"I'm sorry, but Ms. Hamilton has left for the day," said the secretary. "You may leave her a message on her voice mail if you wish."

Jim hung up the phone. Inside, he seethed like a boiling kettle. He knew that woman seemed a bit too poised, too proper, too well dressed to be a simple schoolmate of Kathy's. Now she had coerced him into confessing his thoughts, his innermost secrets, everything for the world to see. His whole life was plastered on the front page of the *Bakersville Gazette* to be trumpeted across the state and beyond. Unending calls for interviews would flood his home once again. People would flock to his doorstep or hover on the street, waiting to catch a glimpse of the poor man who lost his wife. It would happen all over again, like it did a year ago.

"I'm gonna sue that newspaper for all they're worth," he shouted in anger, wadding up the paper and tossing it into the garbage. "They'll pay for this, especially that conniving wench who marched in here, pretending to be someone else. She had no right, invading my privacy." Jim collapsed with exhaustion on the couch. The phone rang several times, but he ignored it. More reporters were undoubtedly itching for interviews. He would have to endure another media frenzy, all because of Leah Hamilton.

When Claire arrived that evening with beef stew for dinner,

Jim refused to even speak to her. He stayed buried in his basement office, surfing the Internet, ignoring her plea to eat. In frustration, he whirled around in his office chair and glared at her. "Quit treating me like a kid."

"Well, when you act like one. . ." She paused and held up the evening paper she had brought. "I'm sorry, Jim, but you have to talk about this."

"I did talk, and look what happened."

"I know. I read the article. How come you let a reporter in the house?"

"I had no idea she was a reporter. She came posing as a long-lost high-school buddy of Kathy's. She had her lines down good. What an actress." He punched the keys on the keyboard. "I'm gonna sue that newspaper. There are laws against invading privacy."

"Did you read the article, Jim?"

"No, I did not. She got it under false pretenses. I'm not going to read how she butchered my words and spread it to the world."

"I thought the article was quite moving. I cried."

"Big deal. So she can move you to tears. That's the way of all reporters. Deception and manipulation."

"I know her tactics were wrong, but she probably knew if she came as a reporter, you would have denied her an interview. And being from the *Gazette,* she knows what happened between you and that reporter named Chet a year ago."

"Yeah, they'll do anything for a story. Act cheap and be cheap."

"Jim, c'mon."

"Just leave me alone, Claire. Stop pestering me for once in your life."

Jim heard the sighs of exasperation as Claire took off down the hallway and up the stairs. Moments later, he heard her bang out the front door, leaving him alone in his misery. Jim slumped in his seat. He felt weak and rundown, exhausted by the daily battles he waged. He swiveled in his chair to see the front page of the *Gazette* staring up at him from where Claire had dropped it on the floor. With mechanical motions he picked it up and scanned the article.

No one can begin to imagine the pain and anguish radiating in the heart of Jim Richards. He married his college sweetheart after promising to provide a good home for her with his computer sales job, hoping that she would remain home with the children. But the children never came, for a bullet stole away not only his wife, but also their first child in what would have been a fairytale ending for this loving couple.

Jim couldn't help but blink back the tears. At least this Leah Hamilton had listened carefully to his story. She had taken his words to heart, writing in a way that described the pain vividly. She went on, detailing with accuracy his frustration at the inability to find the killer, and ending with the memory of a woman devoted to the care of others. Jim placed the paper on the desk. Despite her deception in obtaining the interview, her writing depicted the truth he carried deep within. Yet he would never forgive her for what she had done. Leah Hamilton was deceptive, manipulative, and one who went to the extreme to uncover everything about his life. He vowed she would pay for what she did, somehow, someway.

five

"Ms. Hamilton, I couldn't be more pleased with how this turned out. You're a natural."

Leah Hamilton beamed with pride as she sat before the desk of Mr. Sanders while he scanned her report. Strewn across his desk were multitudes of messages praising her work and that of the paper.

"While I consider your piece more of an opinion than investigative reporting, I'm grateful you were able to accomplish the interview in such a short length of time." He peered over the top of his reading glasses. "How did you manage it?"

"Oh, it took some very careful planning," she said. "I began in the archives, like you said, and sought out the opinions of neighbors who live near Richards's home. I suppose a bit of ingenuity combined with luck." Her hands flew in the air. "Presto, an interview."

"I'm very impressed, and that isn't easy to do. Since you have a knack for opinion pieces, Ms. Hamilton, I was wondering if you would consider a position in the op-ed section of the paper."

Leah lifted her eyebrows. "Meaning what, Sir?"

"Meaning I would like to offer you the position of editorial lead in the paper's editorial section. I've been a little disappointed in the person currently occupying the position. I think with your abilities, this job is right up your alley."

Leah mulled over the proposition. *I could be a real-life editor and even write my own opinions.* It seemed almost unreal. "Thank you, Mr. Sanders. I'll take it."

"Excellent. You may start immediately."

Leah shook his hand before leaving the office. She nearly

danced her way down the hall after the news of her promotion. "This is it! A year-plus at this post, then I'm on my way to the big leagues. I'll have the credentials to back me up and everything!"

When she arrived in her office, the phone rang. "*Bakersville Gazette*, Leah Hamilton speaking."

"So what does the boss think?"

"Chet, what do you want?"

"I read your piece. How you managed to snag the interview is beyond me. I'm sure you are now hailed the queen of the impossible interview."

Leah plastered a hand over her mouth to keep from giggling. "You may be right. For your information, Mr. Sanders just promoted me to editor of the opinion page."

"Really. Interesting."

"So you'll be hearing my opinions a lot in the coming weeks. In fact. . ." She took up a pencil and began rapping it on the desktop. "I might even run an exposé on your little paper. . .perhaps how it lacks the authority to find out the real issues involving our state, especially by a reporter named Chester A. Frazier."

"Ha! No one has even heard of the small paper I work for."

"So I didn't fool you?"

"Not for a minute. But you have charmed me by your diabolical thinking. So how about dinner tonight at Celeste's Italian Ristorante? I want to hear firsthand how you obtained this elusive interview."

"Mr. Frazier, I've told you many times that I think—"

"It's Chet, and I know what you've told me. I've also told you that I'm a persistent person. Obviously, you possess a bit of persistence yourself. So what's wrong with two persistent types persuading each other to enjoy an Italian feast?"

"Chet, you're impossible!"

"I'll pick you up at seven. And yes, I know where you live, so don't worry about giving me directions."

The phone clicked in her ear. Leah tossed the receiver back with an irritated sigh, wondering what she had done to link herself up with such a man. Perhaps an innocent meal and a dagger-eyed look might be enough to chase him away, though she doubted it. She had seen his type before. Not long ago, an editor of a magazine made numerous advances after she went to dinner with him. Leah promptly cleared the air before the situation developed into something she would regret. Chet Frazier held to a set of similar characteristics—arrogance mixed with persistence. "He'll find out soon enough that I don't intend to play his game."

Her telephone rang. She swiped it up to hear the secretary's voice. "Outside call, Ms. Hamilton."

This is it. I'm telling that bird off right now. The phone clicked. "All right, Chet, I've had just about enough of you."

"Excuse me, do I have the right number?"

Oh, no! What if this is some bigwig from a national paper or a television network? "Excuse me, I thought you were. . . never mind. Yes, you've reached Leah Hamilton. How may I help you?"

"I was looking for Sally Johnson."

A tremor shot through her. She gripped the receiver. "Excuse me?"

"Sally Johnson. I heard she worked for you."

"Oh, that Sally Johnson. I'm sorry, she isn't here. Can I take a message?"

"You can quit with the masquerade for one thing," the voice snarled. "I know what you did, and I intend to broadcast your little ruse all over this town. I'll run you out of there so fast, it'll make your head spin."

Leah gasped. Her hands began to shake. "N–Now, Mr. Richards, let me explain why I—"

"There's nothing to explain. Go ahead and write up a juicy story about how I threatened you on the phone, but I intend to spread the same dirt about you. I'll get ahold of all the neighboring papers and trash your well-respected name. You won't be able to walk down the street when I get done." The phone clicked in her ear.

Numbed, Leah slowly replaced the receiver. A terrible feeling came over her, like a ship sinking beneath the waves. *Oh, no. What have I done?* She sunk her head into her arms, thinking of the encounter with Jim Richards in the living room, watching the pain unfold as he described his life. Now the knife of betrayal she had driven into his heart had sent him on a path of revenge. *What am I going to do?*

❧

"Forget about it," Chet said matter-of-factly, stabbing at an olive from a large antipasto dish set between them. Soothing Italian music serenaded them, while the spicy aroma of Italian food wafted from the kitchen. A drippy candle with a tiny flame illuminated their faces.

"I can't forget about it. You should have heard him. He vowed to trash my name all over town. He'll tell everyone I lied to get the interview."

Chet shrugged his shoulders. "So what? Everyone lies and cheats to get ahead in this world. It's nothing new, Leah. You're kicking yourself for this, yet you did nothing but obtain a story for the readers. I know the readers are very forgiving."

Leah poked a tiny fork at a piece of provolone drizzled with Italian dressing. She chewed thoughtfully, wincing at the memory of Jim's voice in her ear. "I just finished hearing about his turmoil, and now I've heaped on more. I should've gone about it in a different way."

Chet placed his fork on the table, folded his hands, and stared at her. "Look, before that character called, you were basking in the glow of a promotion and not having a care in the world how you got it. Then Richards calls and *wham*, you think you've ruined yourself and everyone else. Honestly, Leah, you're a reporter. Reporters go to extremes to get the news. Some bribe others, some masquerade as you did. This is the world. You have to get the news any way you can." He smiled as he resumed eating. "It's just too bad I didn't think of a masquerade to get an interview with Richards. I give you an A plus for smarts, Sweetheart."

Despite his compliment, Leah felt no better about the situation. She dragged herself through the dinner hour, sharing in a plate of lasagna she had no desire to eat. Chet kept the conversation light and humorous with tales of his first job as a journalist and other stories. When the evening was over, Leah thanked him for trying to uplift her spirits.

"You'll get over it," he assured her as he drove her back to her apartment. "Sleep on it. When you wake up to a new day, you can say—'I'm now the editor of the opinion page. If I want, I can write an opinion about Jim Richards and how he's likely the one the cops should be focusing on and not some John Doe walking the street.' "

"Chet," Leah protested, though at this moment she began to wonder if Jim could somehow be involved. Yet the look of anguish on his face during the interview told a different story—of a man caught in a deep depression because there was no justice in this world. Leah had been there. She understood all too well what it meant.

Chet noticed her stark silence. "Well, you never know." He trailed a finger up her smooth arm. "Honestly, just let the man go. You did your job. Your boss is happy. You have a promotion. You aren't the loser, Leah, he is." Chet leaned over and kissed her lightly on the lips. "Wow, I feel like I'm a winner. Good night."

"Good night." Inside the apartment, Leah kicked off her heels and collapsed on the couch. Strewn across the coffee table were news clippings, the tape recorder, and a rough draft of the conversation she had with Jim. She lifted the notepad to read her notations made after the interview. Leah closed her eyes, imagining herself in Jim's shoes with someone posing as a friend from the past, trying to obtain personal details about a loved one's life. "I didn't go about this the right way," she said aloud. "I'd never want someone to do that to me. I have to make amends, but how?"

Leah thought for a moment, then went and picked up the phone. An answering machine came on. "Mr. Richards, this is Leah Hamilton. I wanted to apologize for what I did to you. I hope you will forgive me. Thanks." She replaced the receiver, yet did not feel any better about the situation. "He won't forgive, and he won't forget." She sighed. "He won't forget that I inflicted damage to his wife's memory by posing as a long-lost friend when, in fact, I wasn't." Leah leaned her head against a pillow. "I wish I could live that day all over again and do it the right way." She sat up then and reached for the phone.

"Trish, I've got to talk. You won't believe what's going on." An hour later, Leah was still chewing on a fingernail, which she swore never to do, confiding in her high school chum. Trish was a cosmetic consultant who helped Leah select her wardrobe and suggested ways to improve her appearance.

"What you need is a good facial," Trish told her. "You'd feel better."

"I've already had my mask on, posing as Sally Johnson," Leah said, sighing.

"I agree with Chet. Get on with your life. You have to do your job the best way you know how. Let it go."

"Let it go," Leah repeated. Despite the suggestions made by well-meaning friends, she couldn't.

❧

From the moment Jim threatened her over the phone, Leah was pestered with phone calls by neighboring papers, asking about the interviewing techniques she had used on him. Several opinion pages in other newspapers trashed her ethics as a reporter out to get the scoop, no matter the harm brought upon a grieving man. As hate mail filled the inboxes at the *Bakersville Gazette*, Leah lost all joy in her work. She felt branded a raptor with claws ready to rip into some helpless victim and cause further suffering. The more she thought about it all, the more depressed she became. Chet tried his best to elevate her mood. He sent her a stuffed rabbit with a basket of chocolates, a bunch of balloons, even a huge card that, when she opened it, had a massive chin burst forth with the words, *Keep your chin up*. Leah appreciated what Chet was trying to do, but his efforts felt like a bandage plastered over an infected wound.

Mr. Sanders grew irate by all the mail filtering into the establishment and finally called her in for a meeting. Leah sat stiffly in the chair before his desk as she had numerous times in her past, though this time it was not for glory. The Proverbs picture stared down at her like a disapproving parent. Under the Scripture's glaring eye, she felt like dirt. *Trust in the Lord, not in yourself.* All she had done was trust in her instincts and her ideas. She tried to dismiss the conviction radiating in her spirit, but could not.

"I am deeply disappointed about the tactic you used to gain the interview with Mr. Richards," Sanders snapped. "This is showing poorly on the *Gazette*. We are a reputable paper, you realize. We're receiving many calls from furious subscribers, asking why our paper is continuing to interfere in the life of Jim Richards. Some have cancelled their subscriptions."

"Mr. Sanders, I only did what I felt I needed to in order to—"

"You knew the man was irate about reporters. He was a walking time bomb. I gave you the job of interviewing him simply because I thought you had the skill to find the facts without causing problems. Now you've buried our paper in a muddle of angry readers' mail. Even other papers are accusing us of unethical practices."

"Then I will resign immediately," Leah said, quickly rising to her feet.

He looked at the faxes and other papers scattered across his desk. "I'm sorry, but under the circumstances, I'm forced to do something to show the public that the paper is upset over what a member of our news staff has done. All this clamor forces me to seek your resignation, for the dignity of the paper."

Leah made for the door, keeping her face averted so Sanders could not see the tears hovering in the corner of her eyes. "You'll have my resignation in less than an hour."

"Ms. Hamilton, this is in the best interest of the *Gazette*. I hope we've all learned a valuable lesson from this."

Yeah. Lying doesn't pay. Leah headed straight for her office, ignoring the assortment of stares she received along the way. Once inside, she began emptying desk drawers and file cabinets. Into a plastic garbage bag went pencils, mugs, notepaper, books, and breath mints. She swiped off the pictures from the wall that heralded confidence and faith with a waterfall cascading over a rocky precipice and an eagle soaring high into the deep blue sky. "What a hoot," she snapped, tossing the pictures into the trash. She dried her eyes on the jacket of her suit, knowing the stains she was creating on the linen fabric. "Nothing matters anymore. I was only trying to do what I'm supposed to do. I did nothing to hurt that man personally. I thought I gave him a good article." She plopped down in the chair for the last time and closed her eyes. Jim's angry voice only reverberated in her mind.

I intend to spread the same dirt about you. I'll get ahold of all the neighboring papers and trash your well-respected name. You won't be able to walk down the street when I get done.

"He did it too. Jim Richards got what he wanted: me on a fence post with an unemployed sign hanging around my neck." Her hands ruffled through her long hair. "What's it gonna take to make him to believe that I'm not his sworn enemy? His enemy is that murderer, wherever he is. That killer is the one who's ruined his life and mine!" Leah drew up her chair before the computer and hastily spit out a resignation, which she signed with a flourish. "Good-bye,

Gazette. Good-bye, writing career. Good-bye, life." She left the document sitting on her desk, then made for the door, brushing past coworkers who stared at her in puzzlement. Even the sight of Sam Warner with his mop and pail failed to rattle her nerves.

"Where are you headed off to this early in the morning, Ms. Hamilton?"

Leah painted a thick smile on her face. "Well, Sam, you're in luck. I've been fired."

His eyebrows raised. "You've been fired! No way."

"Of course. No one wants a criminal on his staff. So it's good-bye and good riddance. You'll have to find some other dame to pester." Leah felt a small measure of comfort at the stunned look on the custodian's face, as if he couldn't believe what had happened. Leah pushed open the door to the office and headed out into the bright sunshine. The warm summer air brushing across her face did little to ease her internal turmoil. She thought of all the terrible things she wanted to do to Jim Richards, like writing a nasty note or sending him cockroaches in a candy box. Her pace increased along the sidewalk. The plastic bag containing her belongings grew heavy in her clenched hand. She finally reached her car and threw the bag in the back seat, oblivious to the contents that spilled out inside the immaculate interior. Angry tears slipped down her cheeks, smearing her mascara. For the first time in her life, the confident and poised Leah Hamilton felt like human debris.

Her foot hit the accelerator with a vengeance. Roaring down the street, she passed the different restaurants where she and Chet had eaten together. She thought of the lanky reporter and how he had come to her rescue many times with a word of encouragement. "Chet's right. Jim probably was involved in his wife's death somehow. He's mean enough to do it." She drove out of town and into the suburbs.

Suddenly she heard the whirl of a siren. Flashing white

lights illuminated her rearview mirror. Her eyes darted to the speedometer. "Oh, no," she groaned and brought the car to the shoulder.

"Going a little fast there, aren't you?" asked the county police officer who peered inside her window, scanning both Leah and the interior of the car. "I clocked you going fifty-five in a forty-mile-an-hour speed zone."

"You'd be driving like that too, if you'd just gotten fired," she mumbled before straightening in her seat. "Yes, I suppose I was speeding. I'll add that to my list of faults."

"Hmm." He tipped his hat back. "Well, I'm sorry, Miss, but being fired is no excuse for speeding. It puts your life and everyone else's in danger. I'll need to see your driver's license and registration, please."

Leah groaned. She fumbled for her handbag and thrust the plastic card into his outstretched hand. "Here." She opened up the glove compartment. "You can have this too."

He scrutinized the documents. "Leah Hamilton. Are you the same Leah Hamilton who wrote those news stories about the elementary shooting?"

"Sorry to say, but I am."

"I read the stories. The writing made my wife cry."

He shuffled off to run a check on her license. Leah sat still in her car, her frustration suddenly calmed by the thought of her writing stirring up other emotions besides anger.

The officer returned. "It's all over the news, how you impersonated a friend of Jim Richards's deceased wife in order to gain an interview with him."

"Guess my life is an open book for all to see. Yes, it was totally dishonest. I tried apologizing. It didn't work. The boss fired me. You'll probably read that in the paper tomorrow."

The officer stood silent for a moment before scratching his head beneath his hat. "Ms. Hamilton, I was on duty the day the call came about the school shooting."

Immediately Leah forgot her own troubles. She leaned

closer to the car window. "So you were one of the officers on the scene?"

"In fact, I helped map out the crime scene and rope off the area with the yellow tape. It was the toughest day of my life, let alone my career—kids screaming like crazy, and the teacher lying there. To tell you the truth, I can see why Mr. Richards has had a hard time."

"Why? What do you mean?"

"I mean his wife lay there with a bullet wound in her chest. She was calling her husband's name, telling everyone who helped her how much she loved him. I'll never forget that day, as long as I live."

Leah gaped at the officer's words.

"How any man can go through what he went through, and still have the case unsolved. . .I'm a family man. I love my wife. I couldn't bear to think. . . Anyway, I'll let you go on the speeding this time, Ms. Hamilton. Just don't do it again, or I'll have to write you up a ticket."

"Thanks again, Officer. . . ?"

"Officer Clark."

"Thank you very much, Officer Clark." Leah pulled out into the highway with the officer's heartbreaking description branded in her mind like a hot iron. No matter what Jim Richards had done to her, she couldn't let this all go, not while she still had two feet, two hands, a brain to work with, and a heart open to the pain of others. She was now involved in it all, and with Jim Richards.

six

The encounter with the policeman only fired Leah up in the week following her dismissal from the *Gazette*. Instead of scanning want ads for employment, she surfed the Internet, reading old accounts of the school shooting from various news organizations. Somehow the plight of Jim Richards moved her unlike anything else. For all intent and purpose, she should be bitter toward him for destroying her life. Maybe it had been a blessing in disguise. Leah knew the reason for her interest. Like Jim, she had been wounded by injustice in her past. If only she could communicate to him that she understood a little of what was going on inside him. But she knew he would have nothing to do with her, and likewise, she felt she must keep her distance. Now at the computer monitor, she scrolled down through the additional information she had found on the Taylor School shooting.

Jim Richards was notified of his wife's injury during a conference of computer gaming experts. He arrived at the emergency room of the regional hospital to find that his wife had already died of a gunshot wound to the chest. When asked for a comment, he only shook his head and whispered, "I didn't even have time to tell her good-bye."

Leah winced at these words. She continued to scan the information until a minor detail caught her attention.

No suspects have been found in the recent Taylor Elementary School shooting in which a teacher, Kathy Richards, was gunned down while her students played at recess. The slain teacher's husband, Jim Richards, is reportedly asking the police department to bring in FBI agents to assist in the case but was told that the department would handle the case. Mr.

Richards has denied comment concerning his lack of confidence in the Bakersville Police Department. Friends close to Richards say he is having a difficult time coping with the loss of his wife. They have urged him to seek professional counseling to help with his grief, but he has refused all assistance. Richards's sister, Claire Richards, is assisting with the bereavement process.

"Claire Richards," Leah mused. "Maybe she's someone I could talk to." Leah hunkered down and scanned the computer for more information about the sister. *The victim's sister-in-law, Claire Richards, a deeply religious person, has taken charge of all interviews and reports concerning her brother.* Leah took up a pencil and jotted this down. Another article read, *Claire Richards, sister of Jim Richards, will hold a press conference later today to comment on the progress of the investigation. She is expected to also tell reporters how her brother is coping with the aftermath of his wife's tragic death.*

"There's a lot on this Claire," Leah observed. "It appears she took control of the situation after Jim was unable to cope with it all." Leah's gaze drifted to the ceiling. "I wonder. . ." She mulled over the information. Could Claire Richards hold the key to this bereaved man? After all, the papers said she was religious. Leah had attended church in her past, but she didn't consider herself one of those religious types who stood out in the street, handing out tracts or picketing some social event. After her sister's death long ago, Leah had no interest in God either. However, maybe this one time she would make an exception. Leah continued reading until she found the name of the pastor and the church Claire attended. She could try worming her way into the Richards family by attending their church this coming Sunday and finding out more about Claire and Jim. Leah turned off the computer for the night and hurried to bed. Even with a ray of hope, tomorrow would still be a difficult day.

❧

Leah stared at her reflection in the rearview mirror of her car for the umpteenth time while parked in an obscure corner of the church lot. She smoothed her wavy brown bangs across her forehead and tucked the rest of her hair behind a headband. The last thing she wanted was to have someone in Jim's own church recognize her as the lady fired by the newspaper for deceiving their friend. Leah watched the variety of people who made their way into the homey brick church. Women in summer dresses clutched the hands of their children as they made their way to the entrance. Many walked with a swiftness to their step, tightly holding their Bibles, as if eager to participate in the service.

Leah shook her head, wondering how anyone could be excited about going to church. She had grown up with memories of long-winded church services that left her bored to tears. Often she doodled on paper while the cleric droned on about some meaningless part of life. At times, she stared at the sunlight streaming through the fancy stained-glass windows, painting a variegated picture on the opposite wall. To her, God was a church building, a stained-glass window, or a cold, impersonal statue without emotion that matched the somber mood of the congregation. Yet as she surveyed this congregation, these people were different. They greeted each other with hugs and smiles, talking a mile a minute about their lives. They clung to their Bibles as if the books were a part of them, like a hand or a foot.

When her digital watch gave her two minutes until the start of the service, she prayed no one would recognize her. With her high heels clicking across the blacktop, she hoped beyond hope that Jim would not be there among the faces.

A young strawberry blond woman with a bright smile greeted her in the church foyer. She held out a bulletin, which Leah took. "Welcome! Glad you could come."

Leah smiled. "Thanks." She tried to scoot by, only to find

someone touching her arm. She spun around in a start.

The woman perused her. "Is this your first time visiting us?"

"Yes, it is."

"I'm Claire Richards."

Claire Richards! I've been led right to her! Leah felt her adrenaline soar. "Pleased to meet you. I'm. . ." Leah paused. Suddenly she began to panic. *I can't tell her my name*! "It's great to be here," she said, quickly regaining her composure. "So when does everything start?" The strum of guitars filtered into the foyer. Leah turned to the doors. "Sounds like they're starting already."

"Would you like to sit with me?"

"Well. . .uh, I guess so." Leah followed Claire to seats in the middle of the sanctuary, conscious of the curious eyes staring at her. A sudden thought crossed her mind. *What if Jim is here? What if he recognizes me?* Her hand instinctively went to her hair.

Leah breathed a sigh of relief when she found Jim absent among the attendees. Four guitar players strummed out a lively tune of praise, accompanied by the beat of drums. Her gaze focused on the congregation, watching many of the people closing their eyes and singing. Others raised their hands and praised God. A strange sensation filled Leah. Never had she seen people actually enjoy church music. They weren't bent over thick songbooks, staring blankly at the words, looking as if they couldn't wait for the song to end. The melody enveloped the people until they became one with the music. When Claire stood to join in the worship, Leah reluctantly came to her feet as well, trying to sing while battling the discomfort raging within. *Just think, you're getting to know Claire.*

The uneasiness continued until the music stopped and everyone sat. The pastor walked to the front of the congregation and encouraged all newcomers to stand and be recognized. Leah felt a hard lump grow in her throat. She didn't care to be made a spectacle in front of all these people, especially after the fiasco that involved a member of their congregation.

Again Leah felt Claire patting her arm. "It's all right," she said in a soothing voice. "We just want to get to know you."

"Honestly, I'd rather sit, if that's okay." She smiled weakly, yet knew others were perusing her with curious eyes, as was Claire. When the call came forth to collect the tithes and offerings, Leah reached inside her purse and withdrew her checkbook. She slipped a check inside and passed the basket to Claire. Claire stared with wide eyes and parted lips, as if she were ready to make some comment. The look made Leah increasingly uncomfortable. After the service, Leah hastened for the exit, realizing she had made a terrible mistake by coming. Claire or no Claire, she would never go through this ordeal again.

Behind her came the sound of heels pattering across the hard pavement. She turned to find Claire racing after her with an outstretched hand.

"Please wait! I wanted to give you this. It's a booklet about our church."

"Oh, thanks." Leah stuffed the booklet into her purse.

"I'm glad you came today."

Leah lifted an eyebrow. "Really?"

"Yes. I don't understand everything, but I know God has His ways. He has actually drawn many reporters like you to the church. Some have even accepted Jesus in their hearts. I guess it's true when the Bible says that everything works together for good."

Leah gulped when she heard this. "R–Reporters like me?"

"Yes." Claire stood silent for a moment.

Leah tensed. "Okay, so you know who I am."

A smile lit Claire's face. "Ms. Hamilton, even if I didn't know who you were, God knew."

"What, did God tell you or something?"

"I knew there was something different about you. During the offering, I saw your name in your checkbook." They walked together to the rear of the parking lot where Leah's car stood. "I know you've had troubles with my brother," Claire continued. "I'm sorry about that. I read the article you wrote about him, and I thought it was very touching."

Leah tripped on a small stone and nearly lost her balance. "Huh?" she managed to croak.

"You have a great gift. I know maybe you didn't interview Jim the way you should have, but your words more than made up for it, in my opinion."

Leah fiddled with the strap to her purse, unable to believe what she was hearing.

"Unfortunately, Jim doesn't see it that way. He has bad feelings toward reporters of any kind, and. . ."

"That's what I figured. But you can tell him that he doesn't have to worry about me snooping around any more. I was fired from my job."

"I heard."

"Yes, because of the whole escapade, my boss let me go. So there's no more Sally Johnson. For now I'm just plain old Leah Hamilton, currently unemployed. Jim promised to do me in, and he succeeded. He can wear me like a medal on his chest, proclaiming victory over a dreaded foe." Leah whirled to open the car door.

"Leah, I'm very sorry things turned out this way," Claire said. "I wish Jim wouldn't be so vindictive. He used to be such a nice guy and a wonderful brother. He and Kathy were so in love. When she died, something in him died too. I wish there were some way to bring him back again. He's like a flower that withered and died. He needs God's love. If only he would open up his heart again. That's my prayer."

Leah's fingers froze on the car door while she pondered these words. "Claire, I've done a lot of probing into this whole thing. I've learned some things that have nearly broken my heart. I just wish your brother would forgive me and go on." She slipped inside, casting a quick glance at Claire's solemn face through the driver's window.

"Leah, I totally agree. I wish I knew what to do. I would give anything to have my brother back again, no matter what it takes." Claire took a piece of paper from her purse. "Here's my number. Please call me sometime. Maybe we can have lunch and talk some more."

Leah took the paper through the open car window and perused it. She glanced back to see Claire returning to the church building with her head hanging low, the soft tendrils of her strawberry blond hair dancing in the summer breeze. Leah shifted the car into drive and sped off. Despite the church service that rattled her nerves and the strange meeting afterward, she felt a sense of accomplishment, as if her plan had been the right thing to do.

When she arrived back at the apartment, a silver-colored vehicle sat parked in the space beside hers. A man sat behind the wheel, wearing shades. Leah zipped into the parking place, only to find the man opening the car door and rising to his six-foot height. A smile spread across his face.

"Don't you look nice. Where have you been?"

"Where all people go on Sundays, Chet," Leah said saucily. She flashed him a look of irritation but couldn't help noticing his outfit of a designer-name white polo and shorts that accentuated the tanned hue of his skin. Muscular legs and arms displayed the physique of one who exercised regularly. She drew in a quick breath. "You look like you're ready for Wimbledon."

He laughed. "Not quite, but you're right on one account. I'm heading over to the tennis courts at the country club to hit a few balls. Care to join me?"

"The country club! Since when does a reporter make enough money to join a country club?"

"It was a good deal a few months back. Haven't you ever received offers to join the country club if you sit and listen to their boring talk for ninety minutes?"

"I remember a call awhile back about buying a time-share.

A lady offered me either a miniature television the size of a tennis ball or a free weekend at a motel on the beach if I came to hear the sales pitch."

"Bingo. Mine was for a membership in this country club. I got the free portable television. Anyway, they were running a good deal, so I bought a year's membership. Swimming, sauna, tennis. . ." He swung his arm in the gesture of hitting a ball with a tennis racket. "So how about it?"

Leah shook her head. "I don't play tennis. Besides, I need to scan the Help Wanted."

"Yeah, I heard. Tough break. Maybe I can get you a job with me." His dark eyes glinted in the sunshine, staring with an expression that left her feeling uneasy.

"Enjoy your tennis outing," she managed to say.

"So there's no way I can convince you to come with me? I'm a very good teacher. Exercise helps to ward off stress."

"Thanks, but I really need to do a few things."

As they walked toward her apartment, she fumbled for the keys inside her purse. The church booklet fell out. Chet swiped it up and studied the front cover. "Aha, so that's where you've been. I should have guessed. Claire Richards's church."

"Give that back, please," Leah said, reaching for it.

Chet held the booklet high above his head. "Not so fast. I take it you're continuing with your game plan concerning Richards. Why, pray tell?"

"That's none of your business."

"Isn't it? You made it my business when you came boo-hooing about your problems with Richards. Now I'm conveniently left out? I don't get it. And he's the one who threatened you."

Leah succeeded in stealing the pamphlet out of his surprised hand. "I leave you out when you keep interfering with my life."

Chet twisted his lips into a frown. "I warned you what would happen with this guy, Leah, and you wouldn't listen.

Now you've got the kook threatening you and everything. Why don't you let this go?"

"I can't. No matter how much I try, I can't let that man go. The only reason he threatened me is because he doesn't have the real murderer behind bars. Somehow, the person who killed his wife has to be found."

"Right. So Detective Leah Hamilton plans on solving a crime that has eluded the police department for over a year?"

Her eyebrows lifted at the deep chuckle forming in his throat. "I didn't say I was going to solve it. I don't know anything about it. But I think Jim would feel better if the real criminal were found. He wouldn't be forced to displace his anger on others, like me for example. Anyway, you'd better get going, Chet. The tennis courts are getting cold."

Leah thrust the key into the lock, opened the door, and slammed it shut behind her. Through a side window, she watched Chet stride to his car and climb in. He sat in the driver's seat for several minutes, staring at her apartment with a look that sent a strange sensation flowing through her. When he finally left, his last question tumbled through her mind. *Why don't you let this go, Leah? What do Jim, Claire, and the whole sad scenario of the Taylor shooting have to do with your life?*

"Everything," she declared with a sigh.

seven

Jim felt life couldn't be any worse than it was right now. Ever since the escapade with Leah, he felt himself sinking deeper into a pit of depression. His sales of computer programs had taken a drastic tumble in the last few months, leaving him little in the way of a commission during the second quarter. When he sat down to figure out his budget, he found a shortfall, requiring him to delve into savings to cover living expenses. His boss with Computer Ventures that sponsored his programs warned him that if sales didn't pick up, his contract would be nullified. Jim closed his eyes and sank his head into his arms. Nullified, zapped, liked a roach in contact with a deadly insecticide.

To make matters more uncertain, Claire had been bugging him to make amends with Leah Hamilton. At times, he felt an inclination to follow Claire's suggestion and seek reconciliation. He knew the Bible like the back of his hand. He could recite the Scriptures that told him to forgive. Somehow he couldn't let it go. He only wanted to blame the attractive reporter for his mountain of problems that seemed higher than the summit of Everest.

"Jim, you're being ridiculous," Claire told him earlier that evening after he vented his frustration. She had arrived as always, bringing a pot roast for dinner. Pot roast used to be his favorite dish. Kathy always made it for his birthday and other special occasions. Claire lovingly prepared it with onions, carrots, and potatoes, just the way he liked it. Instead of thanking her and digging into the dish with gusto, Jim gnawed on his lower lip, crossed his arms, and refused to eat it. *The nerve of Claire—making my favorite dish in order to win me over to her side*. The mere thought added fuel to the bitterness stirring within him.

"Leah was just doing her job the only way she knew how."

"By deceiving others? Since when did you decide to support that kind of living? So much for you being a squeaky-clean Christian, defending a liar and a braggart."

Claire lowered her face, turned, and went away, leaving the warm dish of pot roast sitting on the stove. Jim knew he was being unreasonable. Leah was not to blame for his troubles concerning the investigation and his precarious financial state, nor was Claire, for that matter. But he had run out of people to blame in this whole sordid affair. He couldn't blame the killer. The beast remained free, walking the streets, congratulating himself on getting away with murder. If Jim redirected the blame on himself, he feared it would drive him over the edge.

What else could he do but hit hard on the pretty reporter with eyes that melted the icy reservations in his heart? She was attractive, to be sure, with dark eyes that stared inquisitively from a sculptured face. Long fingers and shapely nails had turned the mug of coffee during the interview. Luxurious hair flowed like twin rivers around her shoulders. Again he debated putting aside his anger and calling her. At the last minute he turned away. No, he wouldn't assume the position of a weak-kneed male, looking for forgiveness. She should be here on bended knee, begging his forgiveness.

At that moment the phone rang. Jim fumbled for the receiver and murmured a feeble hello.

"Hello, Jim, this is Mrs. Hanson. Are you all right? You sound terrible."

Jim jerked upright and cleared his throat at the sound of the motherly voice in his ear. "Sure, I'm fine, Mrs. Hanson," he lied.

"I was wondering if you'd like to come over and share some of this nice strawberry rhubarb pie I just made. I went strawberry picking earlier this afternoon at Carson's Farm.

You know that pretty place in the country? It's just beautiful this time of year, and all the fruit is ripe. One of the owner's daughters helped me. These old arms just don't work like they used to. Have you ever been there to pick strawberries?"

Jim shook his head before realizing he was on the phone. "No, I never have."

"You haven't been in my home in so long. I hate to think of you sitting in that big house all by yourself. Come and have a piece of pie, fresh out of the oven. We can have a nice talk. Herb is out tonight, playing cards with his friends. It's lonely."

Jim opened his mouth to reject the offer, but acquiesced instead. He replaced the receiver. A feeling of acceptance came over him at the thought of someone wanting his companionship. He checked his appearance in the bathroom mirror. He ran a comb through his hair. Even if it was Mrs. Hanson, he was glad for the invitation. Things were going no better here, surrounded by these solemn walls and his anger that sucked away life like a leech. He tucked in his shirt and put on a pair of loafers. Maybe, just maybe, God did care, and He had sent Mrs. Hanson to show it.

❧

At the door of the Hanson home, Jim was greeted by the warm smell of pie. The fragrance reminded him of the pies he and Kathy enjoyed during their trip to Maine where restaurants displayed freshly baked blueberry pies on the windowsills of their establishments. One such display beckoned them to enter where they feasted on pie at least four inches thick with fresh blueberries and a hot cup of tea. He walked into the kitchen to find a table set and waiting for him. Mrs. Hanson gave him a warm hug and planted a dry kiss on his cheek.

"I've been so worried about you," she said, serving him a healthy slice of pie.

The delicious fragrance tickled his nostrils. Slices of strawberries and juice trickled out from between the crusts. The saliva swirled in his mouth. Jim forgot his woes and delved into the pie. Nothing in this world tasted so good. The warm food was a welcome relief to his empty stomach. Mrs. Hanson quickly served him another slice while asking about his job.

"I wish business would pick up," Jim commented, scraping the filling off the dessert plate with his fork. "It's so slow right now, I'm barely eking out the income to cover this month's mortgage."

"Will you have to sell the house?"

Jim pushed the plate aside. "Maybe. I hadn't thought seriously about it until now."

Mrs. Hanson sat down next to him and placed a wrinkled hand on his. "To be truthful, Jim, I don't know why you decided to stay in this town. I've had friends who've lost loved ones, you know. They felt the best thing to do was to move away and start fresh somewhere else. Maybe that's what you should do."

"The house would fetch a good price," he mused, "but I really like this neighborhood, and Claire lives here. She's my only family."

"You've been through so much," Mrs. Hanson purred, patting his arm. "If you can't move, then maybe you should think about another lady, Jim. You're still a young man. I know it was hard to lose Kathy, but I think you would do yourself some good if you started seeing other young ladies."

The mere thought of Leah filling that position tensed every muscle in his body. He had considered it, though the thought seemed as far-fetched as snow falling in July.

"So, do you think you will put the house up for sale?" Mrs. Hanson asked.

"Huh? I'm sorry; I was thinking. I'm not sure, Mrs. Hanson. I'll consider it and maybe talk to a Realtor."

They conversed for another thirty minutes while Jim slowly ate his third piece of pie. When the clock struck nine, he bid her farewell and went back to his empty house that felt even colder than he remembered.

Jim ventured down to the basement and his office, hoping to bury his depression on the Internet. He turned the computer on, listening to the machine whirl to life. Suddenly, his eye caught sight of the evening paper from several days ago, and the article by Leah Hamilton, lying on the floor.

Slain Teacher's Husband Speaks Out. After a year of silence, Jim Richards speaks candidly about his experiences in the aftermath of his wife's death.

Jim froze, realizing he had never thrown out Claire's copy of the paper that had caused the rift between Leah and him. He swiped it up, preparing to toss it into the wastebasket, when his eyes again fell on the all-too-familiar words.

No one can begin to imagine the pain and anguish radiating in the heart of Jim Richards. He married his college sweetheart after promising to provide a good home for her with his computer sales job, hoping that she would remain home with the children. But the children never came, for a bullet stole away not only his wife, but also their first child in what would have been a fairy tale ending for this loving couple.

Jim bit his lip. Instead of feeling anger, tears rolled down his cheeks. He sat down with a thud. For months he had entertained himself with depressive thoughts or an angry temperament. There had been no joy or laughter in his life, not even the semblance of a smile. Claire mentioned the permanent frown lines etched in a pattern around his mouth. Jim closed his eyes. He hated the anger and hurt. The grave of sorrow and grief he had dug for himself had sealed him away from life. If he didn't break out of it soon, he feared he might never again see the light of day.

"How do I break out? God, I've lost everything. How can I go on?" With the computer humming before him, Jim inserted a Bible CD and began reading Scriptures that brought healing to his fractured heart. When he was through, he closed his eyes. "God, I'm a mess. I've tried to handle all of this on my own strength. I can't do it anymore. God, I need You to take control. I need You to take away this hate and this bitterness. Please, God, work a miracle in me before it's too late."

❧

Without a job to keep herself occupied, Leah spent much of her time thinking about the meeting with Claire and the Taylor School shooting. At times she considered taking up Claire's offer and calling her, but couldn't find the will to pick up the phone. Perhaps it was Claire's Christianity that bothered Leah, or that fact that Claire was Jim's sister. Yet a part of Leah desperately wanted reconciliation. She hated the idea of someone angry with her because of something stupid she did. She always wanted to make amends before the situation got totally out of hand, like it had with Jim. The apology she left on his answering machine had been a start, but with no word of forgiveness coming from Jim, Leah felt more had to be done.

Numerous times she drove by Jim's home on Elderberry Lane, stopping to observe the framed house and country porch. The lawn had been mowed since the day she and Chet hid under the decking. The front garden bed still lacked flowers to spruce it up. At that moment, a thought crossed her mind. She remembered during the interview that Jim praised his wife's gardening skills. After the comment made by Claire, that Jim was like a dying flower, her mind began churning with ideas. "Maybe that would help mend the fence," she mused. Immediately, she headed to the nearest nursery on the outskirts of town. She would fix this, no matter what the cost.

When she arrived at the garden center, her senses quickly became overwhelmed by the multitudes of flowers and plants for sale. She stared at annuals, perennials, vegetables, and flowering trees. There were plants for full sun, partial shade, and full shade. Leah shook her head. She felt dizzy just looking at all the varieties.

"Can I help you?" asked a matronly woman.

"Yes, please. I would like to put a few flowers in a front flowerbed, but I'm not very good with plants. In fact, I know nothing about them."

"Does the garden receive full sun, partial shade, or full shade?"

"Uh. . . ," Leah paused, thinking about Jim's house and its position relative to the sun. "Does it matter?"

"It most certainly does. There are plants specifically adapted to certain areas of sunlight. If the area receives full sun, it will immediately kill annuals such as impatiens. Vincas and peonies prefer full sun, or they won't bloom properly."

"Wow, I didn't realize that. Okay, I think the bed receives partial shade. The sun shines in the morning, then the bed becomes shady when the sun goes behind the house in the afternoon."

"Come right this way, and I'll show you what we have in stock." The saleslady showed her many different bedding plants, including begonias and impatiens. "Impatiens come in many colors: muskmelon orange, pastel white, lavender, even candy-cane striped. They're very easy to grow and maintain their blooms all summer long."

"I guess I'll take those in a couple different colors," Leah decided. "Now what should I do with them once I get home?"

"Be sure you keep them well watered and in a shady spot until you plant them. Then dig a round hole, deep enough to set the roots in without crowding them. Add a little of this fertilizer," the saleslady directed, placing a box of fertilizer on the counter, "and put some water in the hole. Place the plant inside, then add soil back into the hole and water thoroughly. I would water every day for several days so the plants have time to adapt."

Leah nodded, trying to internalize all this information. She wished she'd brought along her trusty tape recorder. "And they'll grow?"

"The plants may require fertilizing about halfway through the season, depending on the condition of the soil. Since you haven't planted anything there, you may need to add some later."

Leah nodded. "Okay, so how much does this come to?"

The woman took her over to the cash register. "Three packs of plants, a box of fertilizer. . ."

Leah handed her a pair of fine-grained leather gardening gloves and a steel trowel.

"Fifteen dollars and eighty cents."

With her purchases tucked in the rear of the car, Leah drove home to change into dingy jeans and a T-shirt before arriving at Jim's house. She wondered what the neighbors would think if they saw her planting flowers in his yard, but she shoved the thought away. With determination, she walked to the front beds and began digging out the weeds that had grown several feet high, obscuring the row of bushes behind. After a time, her fingers began aching from tugging at the roots. Bushes lining the front of the home slowly began to emerge as she worked. Leah sat back on her heels to admire the job.

"Now the plants," she said, walking to her car to lift out the box of impatiens.

Just then, a distant voice hailed her from next door. "Yoo hoo!" an elderly woman called, waving her hand.

Leah gulped. She managed a weak smile in the elderly neighbor's direction. This is what she feared most—that the neighbors who had defended Jim in the past would find her here and disrupt her plans for reconciliation.

"What are you doing on Jim's property, young lady?"

Leah surprised herself with how easily she launched into her smooth rhetoric. "Oh, I'm a friend. I wanted to surprise Mr. Richards by planting some flowers in the front bed here.

I know his wife loved flowers."

A smile spread across the older woman's face. "Yes, she did. What a lovely thought. Herb and I have been looking at Jim's front bed for a long time. I wish I had the strength to pull those weeds. I'm glad someone is doing it. By the way, I'm Emma Hanson."

"Pleased to meet you." Leah smiled again before marching over to the front beds. She knelt down and began digging the holes for the flowers. To her dismay, Mrs. Hanson followed and hovered over her shoulder, observing her work. Leah measured the width of the hole using one of the plants, then dug the hole with her sparkling trowel, piling the soft, brown earth to one side. She hoped the elderly woman wouldn't notice the trembling fingers inside her leather gloves that soon began to sweat from both labor and anxiety.

"You do a very careful job, dear," Mrs. Hanson noted. "Did you buy those plants from Markman's Nursery?"

"Yes, I did."

"They're very good people. I have plants from them that have lasted me for years. Over there in the front is my prized azalea. You should see it in the springtime. It's the biggest bush on the whole street. Many people drive by just to see it in bloom. I bought it ten years ago, right from Markman's Nursery. It's done beautifully for me."

Leah continued to work as Mrs. Hanson chattered on about her plants and then about Kathy's love for flowers. "I helped her many times with the gardening," Mrs. Hanson recalled. "She wanted to plant a vegetable garden one year. Jim wasn't too happy about it. He didn't want to do all that digging. We lent him the tools, and Herb came over to lend him a hand. You should have seen what kind of garden the two of them had! Tomatoes galore, and the most beautiful squashes. I gave Kathy a recipe for making spaghetti sauce, and she gave me a jar of it for Christmas one year. Would you believe I still have it in the pantry? Now I'm glad I kept it as a reminder. Oh, the poor thing. How I miss her."

With the conversation whittling away the time, Leah planted each impatien, alternating the colors until she found herself finished with the row. "There," she exclaimed in glee, climbing to her feet to observe the effect.

"Beautiful. I'm sure Jim will be surprised indeed. You say you're a friend? I've never seen you around."

"Yes, well, kind of," Leah managed to say as she quickly gathered up her equipment. "It was nice meeting you, Mrs. Hanson."

"Take care, and if you ever want to help me plant flowers, I'd love your assistance. My back just can't take the bending anymore. Good-bye." The lady waved cheerfully as Leah made off for the car.

Before driving down the road, she glanced back for one last look at the home. The flowers gave the place an appearance of love and hope. A lone tear trickled down her cheek. "I hope you'll realize how sorry I am for deceiving you, Jim."

❧

Jim stared in shock and amazement when he pulled into the driveway that evening. The sun had already dipped behind the house, but he could plainly see the row of flowers planted in front of the bushes. The delicate flowers added an innocent beauty he had not seen since Kathy's death. He walked up to the bed and stared down at them. The flowers waved gently in the evening breeze as if to greet him. He sat down in the grass before the garden bed and stroked the velvety petals that reminded him of the many times Kathy lovingly tended the garden. When new flowers would pop open, she would smile and call them her love gifts. Now the warm colors sparked rays of sunshine after months of anger and depression. He sighed, wondering who could have known how much the flowers would mean to him. Jim immediately went inside and called the Hansons.

"It wasn't me, Jim," Mrs. Hanson denied when he thanked

her for his welcome-home gift. "A pretty young lady came by this afternoon and planted them."

"What young lady?"

"She said she was a friend of the family. She knew how much Kathy liked flowers and thought it would do some good to put plants in the front bed. I couldn't have agreed more. Aren't they beautiful? Just the way Kathy would want the bed to look."

Confusion filled him. He poured himself a cold soda. "Did she say her name?"

"Why, no, she never did tell me her name. But she's a very pretty girl. And she planted the flowers with such care! She had everything too—a brand-new trowel, expensive gloves. . ."

"What did she look like?"

"Hmm, let me see. She had on jeans and a T-shirt, I think, with palm trees on it. I don't have the memory I used to. She had dark brown hair, pulled back into a ponytail. A very pretty face, as I've said. Big brown eyes. A nice smile. . .a sunshine smile I call it."

Jim took a swallow of his soda. "She doesn't sound like anyone I know."

"Perhaps she's a teacher friend of Kathy's from school or something."

"Maybe. That's probably it." He relaxed in the kitchen chair. "There were plenty of teachers and parents who liked her very much. Well, that was nice of her. It sure did brighten my day."

"I should say. Anyway, you enjoy them."

"I will. Thanks." Jim replaced the receiver and downed the rest of his drink before placing the glass in the sink. *A woman with dark brown hair and brown eyes.* He mulled over Kathy's acquaintances in the past—the friends she'd invited for coffee or for dinner. No one seemed to match that description, except for the impostor that came to his home a few weeks ago. He recalled vividly the dark, almost black, hair cascading down her shoulders, and intense brown eyes that stared into his. The picture fit Mrs. Hanson's description. Jim suddenly shot to his feet. "It was her. Leah did it. She must have. She remembered what I told her about Kathy—how she had planted flowers just for me." All at once, confusion swirled within him. How was he to treat this? What should he do? He swiped up the phone and called Claire.

❧

Leah stared at the classified section spread out before her, but her mind wasn't on employment. It was on the flowers in Jim's garden and the pleasant conversation with the elderly woman that made the work go so quickly. A sense of community was something foreign to Leah. She had always grown up on the fast track of city life. There was never time for growing plants, friendly chats with neighbors over a cold glass of lemonade, or delving into simple country living. She was always running here and there, performing needed tasks, or trying to get ahead in life. The brief respite she took digging in the rich earth, surrounded by plants and flowers, rejuvenated her heart. Perhaps she should consider nurturing some plants of her own to put a bit of life back into her dreary apartment. Maybe an herb garden in a terra cotta container to spice up a dish or two would be easy enough.

It didn't take long for Leah to return to Markman's Nursery and buy all the things she needed to sow herself a miniature herb garden in a large pot. She couldn't wait for the tiny seedlings to burst forth from the soil. She watered the pot carefully and set it in the sunlight for warmth. From her readings in a book on herbs that she checked out of the library, the seedlings all appeared the same when they first emerged from the ground. The second set of leaves would take on the plants' characteristics—the broad, pungent leaves of basil, curly leaves for parsley, needles for rosemary, and soft velvet for sage. Leah began planning what she would do with the herbs—those she would dry for seasonings or package individually into plastic bags with bright ribbons to give as Christmas gifts.

With the book on herbs and the classifieds spread out next to her, Leah decided to make herself a cup of herbal tea to soothe her raw nerves. She had debated spending so much money on the plants with her budget tightened severely from her lack of employment. She would have to find a job soon or risk waitressing in some cheesy establishment, which she detested. Filling the mug with tap water, Leah wondered how everything in her life could have turned upside down so quickly. At times, she wished she had never taken the job at the *Gazette* but remained content to write profile pieces on famous personalities for the major magazines. Now, she found herself mixed up with flowers, an irate man, a mysterious murder, and unemployment, all because she had taken up the daunting task of writing the anniversary story on the Taylor Elementary School shooting.

The microwave signaled. Leah removed the steaming cup of tea, then rummaged around the cupboard for the honey. Another wrench thrown into the mixture was the persistence of Chet Frazier, who, for some reason, believed they should remain together. Over the course of the week, she'd declined several invitations from him for dinner.

"How are you eating then?" he had asked.

"What's that supposed to mean?"

"I mean, where are you getting the money to feed yourself?"

"I eat just fine, thank you. Please mind your own business."

"You are my business," he had told her before hanging up. The next night, Chet called to say he was having dinner delivered to her apartment. Leah reluctantly accepted the white bags from the deliveryman. The Styrofoam containers that held a sumptuous feast from a classy French restaurant must have cost him half a paycheck. Leah decided it was too much for one person to eat and invited her friend Trish to come over. The two of them sampled the foreign fare while exchanging girl talk at the kitchen table.

"I think Chet's one great guy," Trish declared. "Why be so picky about what he does? It's obvious he's trying every trick in the book to get your attention. You have to love it!"

Leah only wondered what his real motive might be and if anything good would come of it. She stirred honey into the cup of steaming tea, deciding this would be her dinner for the night, when the telephone rang. Leah swirled the spoon around in the fragrant liquid, debating whether to answer the call. Another conversation with Chet might bring her to the edge of insanity, and she didn't need Trish telling her to get over her insecurities. Finally, on the fourth ring she swiped it up with a short hello.

"Is this Leah?" came a female voice.

Leah breathed a sigh of relief, thankful it was not Chet or Trish. "Yes."

"This is Claire Richards. Remember me?"

Leah put down the mug of tea and instinctively reached for a pad and pen. "Of course I remember you. How are you?"

"I'm fine. I was wondering if you were doing anything tonight? I'd like to have you over for dinner."

Leah glanced down at her cup of tea, just as a sharp pain of hunger stabbed her stomach. "Actually, I was going to have my cup of tea here."

Claire laughed. "You can't live on tea."

"That's true."

"Let me give you the directions."

Leah scribbled down the information. "That's not too far from me."

"Great! I look forward to seeing you again. Bye."

Leah hung up the phone, took one look at herself, and dashed off to the bedroom to throw on some decent clothes. She had just put on a pair of pants and a blouse when the phone rang. "Yes?" she said breathlessly, running a comb through her long hair.

"You can't refuse me this time. I'm right here in your parking lot, ready to whisk you away to a leisurely dinner."

Leah groaned out loud. "Oh, Chet, I can't tonight. I've already accepted a dinner invitation."

Silence met her ears until a droll voice came over the receiver. "Oh, really? And who's the lucky guy? Jim Richards?" He laughed shortly.

Leah's face warmed at the mere suggestion. "Of course not, and quite frankly, it's none of your business. I don't need you telling me who I can see or what I'm supposed to do. Now if you'll excuse me, I have to get ready."

"Can't you call up your friend and tell him you have a headache? Or a toothache, perhaps?"

"That would be dishonest. I'm tired of taking that route in life. Besides, I want to go."

"Your loss." The hum of the dial tone filled her ear. It was the first time Chet had ever hung up on her, despite the many nasty things she had said to him in the past. Leah pushed the thought from her mind to ready herself for dinner. Before leaving the apartment, she peeked out the window, searching for Chet's silver sports car in the parking lot. Finding it absent, Leah locked the door and strode over to her own car. A few spaces down stood a rental car with a driver hunkered down in the seat, the face hidden behind the front page of the *Bakersville Gazette*.

❧

Leah arrived at Claire's apartment to find the aroma of Italian food permeating the air. The short woman stood in the kitchen, slicing up the makings for a tossed salad. A small pan on a potholder contained the most appetizing lasagna Leah had ever seen. "I'm so glad you could come on such short notice," Claire said with a smile.

"Thanks for inviting me."

Her face became somber when she pointed to the lasagna. "This was supposed to be for Jim and me, but he couldn't come. Some kind of commitment, he said. I didn't want it to go to waste."

"Do you eat together often?" Leah wondered, sitting down on a stool at a kitchen nook while Claire finished the salad.

"I take dinner over to his house most nights. I make it a point to see him every day if I can."

"It must be hard."

"It's not easy," she admitted, turning to the refrigerator and opening the door to examine the array of bottled salad dressings lining the shelf. "What kind of dressing do you like? I have an assortment in here. It's amazing how much a single woman can collect when it comes to salad dressings."

"I know," Leah said with a smile, recalling the contents of her refrigerator that contained six different dressings, two bottles of mustard, and loads of other condiments that she only served to guests. She relaxed on the stool, thankful to find a bit of similarity between herself and Claire. "I'll have ranch."

Claire snatched up the ranch and Italian bottles, setting them on a table covered with a light pink tablecloth. Carnations with baby's breath stood arranged in a vase. "Your table is very nice," Leah added.

"Thanks. A guy from church gave me the flowers. Rick said I needed a little cheering up in my life. He's been very nice."

"Is he your boyfriend?"

Claire flushed. "Oh no, just a friend."

"Sounds to me like he's making a step forward if he's giving you flowers."

The comment generated a rosy tint in Claire's cheeks. "Well, you see, in our church, we don't do much in the way of dating and such. We trust in God to bring that special man or woman into our lives."

Leah raised an eyebrow. "No dating? Then how do you know if a man's right for you?"

"It all comes from trusting God," she said, placing the lasagna on the table. "I've trusted Him for everything in my life, you see—even with my passport to heaven once I leave this world. If I can trust Him with my life, I know I can trust Him with the man He wants me to marry."

Leah marveled at this while Claire took her place at the end of the table and motioned for her to sit. In view of her battles with Chet, the idea of releasing dating and marriage left a peaceful impression. Leah bowed her head and listened to Claire speak to God in a conversational tone as if He sat at the table with them. Leah picked up her napkin and placed it across her lap. "This looks delicious, Claire."

"I hope you like it." She placed a slice of lasagna on a plate and handed it to Leah. "I really didn't want to eat alone tonight. I don't know how Jim does it. This place would just close in around me. I have to be with someone, whether it's a meeting at church or chatting with someone on the phone."

"I know from the papers that you handled most of the communication during the whole tragedy with Jim's wife."

"I was forced into it. Jim was so bothered by all the media attention, I had to step in and take the burden off of him."

Leah chewed thoughtfully on a portion of lasagna before commenting, "You really care a lot about him, don't you?"

Claire smiled. "He tests me sometimes," she admitted, "but yes, I do. He's my only brother. We've been through so much together. I was one of Kathy's bridesmaids. Kathy and he were made for each other." She put down her fork and stared off into space. "They were good to me, inviting me over, helping me get over this one guy I thought God wanted me to marry. Kathy was very sensitive in that way. I just can't believe someone would do this to her. He must be a madman."

"So the police still have no leads in the case?"

Claire shook her head. "That's probably the saddest thing of all. I've had to release the burden to God's care, or it would be too much to handle. I know I need to forgive whoever did this terrible thing. I don't know how that person can walk on this earth, knowing what he's done. He must be in turmoil, unable to sleep or eat. I only pray that one day God will speak to his heart and he will confess to his crime."

Leah chewed several more bites when the doorbell rang. Claire jumped up to answer it. As Leah's fingers curled around the glass of iced tea, a male voice echoed in her ears. Her hand froze.

"I'm glad you changed your mind," Claire's voice responded. "Come have some lasagna."

Leah turned to see the visitor who stood in the foyer of the apartment. A set of hazel-colored eyes locked with hers. The face belonged to Jim Richards.

eight

They stared at each another, unblinking, for only a moment. Jim shifted his feet. He wanted to leave but forced himself to stay. He fixed his sights on the figure that sat hunched over a bowl of salad, trying in vain to avoid looking at him. He couldn't help but notice the kitchen light reflecting on her luxurious brown hair that cascaded down her back. A smooth hand trembled slightly when the fork stabbed at the salad leaves. A mouth tinted with wine-colored lipstick opened slightly to receive the salad. Leah was beautiful, just as he imagined. Though she didn't know it, over the course of time, her image was replacing Kathy's in his thoughts and dreams.

Jim said nothing as he followed Claire into the kitchen and sat down opposite her. It was the first time they had met since the interview. He trembled for an instant at the way she had deceived him, until he recalled the Scriptures he had confessed. He refused to go back to the old ways of hate. He must now embrace a new way. . .and a better way. . .even if right now he couldn't put the feelings into words. Leah had already suffered for it, and he had as well.

He helped himself to the salad and lasagna while Claire made every effort to engage him in conversation. Soon she became a lone voice echoing at the dining table. Leah said nothing, and neither did he. The silence was unnerving. All during the meal, questions assaulted his brain. Was she the one who had planted the flowers? If so, why? Was she as interested in him as he was in her? He tried to open his mouth to speak, but no words came out.

At last Claire began asking questions, hoping to spur on a conversation. It proved too unnerving. Jim rose to his feet, sensing his presence had dampened the meeting. "Look, I need to go. Thanks for the dinner." They were his only words the entire evening.

"Jim, I wish you wouldn't. . . ," Claire began.

He only drifted away to the front door. When he glanced back, the dark and beautiful eyes of Leah Hamilton met his. There was something in those eyes that stirred him. They held no anger or resentment, but only regret. Jim paused in the hallway of the apartment complex to muse over that face. He plunged his hands into the pockets of his trousers and made for the exit. Almost as swiftly, he turned about and headed back to Claire's door where he paused and pressed his ear to the door. He could hear voices speaking—first Claire, then Leah. He heard faint ramblings, none of it discernible through the closed door. He sighed and meandered off, feeling the sadness grip him once again.

❧

"Thanks for the great meal, Claire." Leah helped her rearrange the table and place a silver bowl of fruit on a crocheted doily.

"I'm so glad you could come. I apologize again for Jim. I don't know what's the matter with him."

"It's all right. I've come to expect it." Claire handed her a cup of herbal tea that felt soothing in Leah's hands. "I've wished a hundred times over I never went by his house, posing as a long-lost friend of Kathy's. I thought planting the flowers in front of his home would help."

Claire sipped her tea. "I know it did something, Leah. He called me when he got home and told me all about them. I even heard from Mrs. Hanson. You touched many people by your thoughtfulness. It was a very nice thing to do. Unfortunately, Jim has a hard time accepting any kind of blessing in his life. His pain is his entire world. When someone tries to barge in on it, he reacts either with hostility or he withdraws, like tonight."

"Could it be that his pain has to do with the fact that the police have never solved the case?"

Claire nodded. "I think it would bring closure if Jim were to see the criminal pay for his crime. Jim lets the anger boil up inside. I've tried to get him to release his anger and allow God to take control of the situation, but he just pushes God away. He hasn't been to church since it happened."

Leah shifted at the reverent words. She never once considered allowing God a free rein in her life. To her, God was a personality hidden far away in the clouds, serenaded by little cupids playing harps. God might be reachable when one was in dire straits, but even then, only in the presence of some minister or priest.

"I found I had to go right to the One who had the strength to deal with the pain," Claire continued. "I mean, after the tragedy, it seemed like I had lost both my sister-in-law and my brother. I cried for days. Sometimes I felt I should have erected a tombstone for Jim right next to Kathy. . .it was that bad."

"So he's really not. . .well, hostile and all?"

Claire shook her head. "Jim's a wonderful guy and an awesome big brother—one who would defend me against the bad guys or would dry the tears from my face if I scraped my knee. When you see him act this way, it's the pain driving him to do it. He doesn't have God in control of his life right now. Jim's flesh is in control."

Leah crinkled her forehead in confusion. "His flesh?"

"His flesh—the part of him that's filled with bitterness, grief, selfishness, anger. When God's in control, there's love, joy, and peace. There's a big difference."

"I guess," Leah said dubiously, wondering if the flesh controlled her. At times she felt loving and peaceful. Now she wondered if these feelings were merely propagated by her own self-interests. The more Leah sat in Claire's presence, the more she yearned for Claire's kind of peace.

Driving home to her apartment that night, Leah ruminated

on Claire's words. Now unemployed and without a plan for the future, the weight of life felt unbearable. The idea of giving one's burdens over to God proved tempting. She wondered how someone went about releasing such burdens. Should she go back to Claire's church on Sunday? Should she speak to a minister, or perhaps offer a simple prayer like the kind she heard at the dinner table? Leah wished she had asked Claire what to do before leaving the apartment.

Leah drove into her apartment complex to find Chet sitting on a park bench, waiting for her. He wore a nice pair of pleated trousers and a white shirt with a colorful tie hanging loose around his neck. "Oh no, not again."

He stood to his feet and waved. "So how was the date?"

Leah brushed by him on her way to the apartment door.

"Guess I'm out and he's in. Is that the final deal?"

"Oh, for heaven's sake," Leah muttered, jamming her key into the front door. "If you must know, I had dinner with Claire Richards."

"You had dinner with Claire Richards?" Chet stepped back as if startled by the statement. "That's a relief. Now I can sleep the night away, knowing you're still safe."

Leah turned, puzzled by his statement. "Safe from what?"

"Safe from other men trying to sweep you off your feet with a candlelight dinner and conversation." He extended his arms. Leah opened the door and shut it in his face with a slight bang.

"Hey, what's the big idea?" he shouted through the closed door.

Leah could not help but crack the door open and grin at him. "Just curious to see your reaction."

"Okay, you saw it. Now come have a cup of coffee with me. I have some great news to tell you."

"Chet, it's getting late. I have to start looking for employment in the morning, or I'll be homeless in a month."

"Look no farther than your front door, Sweetheart. Chester

A. Frazier to the rescue of a beautiful damsel in distress."

"What's that supposed to mean?"

"Have a cup of coffee with me, and I'll tell you."

Leah shrugged and followed him. They drove straight to a small café on Main Street, a few doors down from the deli where she first met him for lunch during her initial inquiry into Jim's life. The mere thought of Jim Richards's prompted a strange feeling inside the pit of her stomach. Once they were seated in a cozy booth, Chet ordered two cappuccinos and two croissants.

"I just had a big dinner," Leah complained.

"A little evening snack," he said with a wink. "So how is Claire doing these days? She is an attractive girl, I must admit. Did I ever tell you I once asked her out?"

"She said she doesn't date."

"I know. She told me. Flat out refused. Can you imagine anyone refusing to go out with old Chet?" A grin rapidly crossed his face. "So how was dinner?"

The waitress came by with their order. Leah sipped on the coffee. "All right. I ran into Jim, though."

"You ran into Richards? I'm sure that was an exciting encounter."

"One for the books. He just sat there and stared, then high-tailed it out of Claire's apartment before I could give him my disease."

Chet snickered. He took up a croissant, broke it in half, and slathered it with butter. Leah cringed in disgust when he stuffed the pastry into his mouth.

"I didn't have dinner," he informed her with a wink. "I was so upset about you going out with someone else, I had no appetite."

"So what's the news?"

"I found you a job."

Leah put down her coffee. "You found me a job? Where?"

"I got you a job at the *Gainsport Herald*. I work for a very low-keyed boss who believes you've done wonders with the school story, despite what everyone else thinks. He's like me . . . . That is, he does whatever needs to be done to get the story out to the readers. He liked your approach with Richards. If you ask me, the *Gazette* is turning out to be too much of a goody-goody, squeaky, Mr. Clean publication. Sanders has lost his touch over the years."

"It's only because he doesn't want criminals on his staff."

Chet smiled. "My boss doesn't care who's on staff, so long as they do the job. In that place, you can have a police record and still find plenty of work to do."

The statement cast a cloud of depression over Leah. Never in her life did she think she would be classified as a criminal.

"Anyway," Chet continued, "I talked with my boss tonight on the phone while you were off dining with Richards's sister. He said to hire you by all means. We'll be working together as a team."

Leah raised her eyebrows. "As a team? Look, Chet, I really prefer to work alone. That's how I operate."

"I told the boss that you might prefer your own reporting, at least until you get settled. But remember, beggars can't be choosers. We need to do whatever he says, for now, anyway."

"Well, thanks for thinking of me. It's a relief not to have to look for a job anymore."

Chet took up her hands in his and gave a gentle squeeze. "Leah, I'm always thinking of you," his deep voice purred. "Day or night, I don't stop thinking of your beautiful face or what I can do to help. You start at the *Herald* first thing tomorrow, bright and early. If you want, I'll even provide you a free escort service for your first day on the job."

"Thanks, but I know where the office is. I'd like to check it out first and see if that's where I'm meant to be."

Chet raised his eyebrows. "Leah, it's a job! Be thankful for the opportunity. I mean, I know it isn't *USA TODAY,* but at least it will put bread on the table. Homeless people don't eat too well unless it's food from the Salvation Army cafeteria."

"I know, Chet, and I'm grateful. I'm just trying to figure out what I'm supposed to do with my life right now. Maybe I'm not cut out to be a reporter."

"If you want my honest opinion, I think you need to get out of this whole school shooting scenario. As it is, our paper has gone on to bigger and better stories. That's the main reason I got you this job. It's time to push Jim, his sister, and everyone else out of the picture and get on with your life. I mean, look what it's done to you emotionally. You used to be so calm and composed. Now you're a nervous wreck. I'll bet you haven't slept well either. Pretty soon you'll be using cigarettes and frequenting the bar scene. Your health will go right down the tubes."

"That's not true," Leah retorted in indignation. "I've never smoked or drank in my life, nor am I about to."

"All I'm saying is, just think of tomorrow as a new beginning to your career. No more Jim or school shootings, just a new job as a classy reporter and maybe even a fresh start for the two of us."

Leah listened, intrigued by the promises at this juncture in her life. Yet she couldn't help but think of Claire's forlorn face that evening and the pain she had described. How could Leah tear herself away from these hurting people? How could she just forget them and forge ahead with her life as though nothing had happened? Wasn't that the picture of selfishness Claire painted at the dinner table? Wouldn't she rather have real peace and joy? The silence continued, even as Chet drove her back to her apartment. Before she could open the car door, he curled his arm around her and drew her close.

"Now I'm supposed to reward you for getting me a job?" Leah asked, trying to wiggle her way out of his embrace.

Chet withdrew and folded his arms across his chest. "Nope. I won't have you thinking I'm only after stolen kisses and not your welfare. I'll wait for you to make the first move."

"You're crazy, you know that?" Leah shook her head, even as the street lamps glowed in his dark eyes. She sat for a moment, considering his handsome features of dark brown hair and a sparkle in his eyes. To her amazement, he seemed willing to yield his brash personality to her pace in the relationship. This did not characterize a man with an ulterior motive, but one who cared about her feelings. With a sigh, she thanked him for the coffee and the job.

"My pleasure." He leaned forward in expectancy. "Anything else I can do for you? Name it."

"Oh, you," she conceded, finally succumbing to the lips that had waited so patiently for her to respond. The contact was tender and soft, a far cry from the kind of man she had witnessed the last few weeks. When they parted, she sighed. "I guess you deserve it. You've always been there, through the good, the bad, and the ugly."

"I work hard," he said with a smile, running a finger across her lips. "Good night, my damsel in distress. And don't worry about transportation in the morning. I'll pick you up for your new job bright and early at seven-thirty, since we have a little drive to Gainsport." He offered another warm kiss on her lips that lingered for nearly a minute, sending a hot flush radiating through her. When they parted, she fumbled for the door handle and hurried into the night air.

"This is unbelievable." Leah floated into the apartment and locked the door behind her with a sigh of contentment, until she saw her herb garden. Beside it rested the steel trowel and the gardening gloves she had used to fix up Jim's garden. Thoughts of Chet and his kiss faded away at the memory of Jim's pained eyes staring at her over dinner.

nine

"You seem nervous," Chet observed. "That's the third time you've opened your purse."

"New-job jitters, I guess." Leah avoided his gaze to concentrate on the scenery outside the car window. She wished at that moment she had driven herself to work. Driving would have focused her mind on morning traffic rather than her first day of work in a new newspaper office. Chet had picked her up promptly at seven-thirty, presenting her with a huge bouquet of red roses for her first day on the job. He waited patiently in the doorway of the kitchen while she snipped off the ends and tucked the long stems into a vase of tepid water. During the night, instead of dwelling on Chet, Leah found herself occupied with thoughts of Jim, Claire, and the shooting. Now she regretted kissing Chet like she had. She hoped it didn't signal to him an interest in a relationship. The last thing she wanted to do was be involved with anyone at the moment.

Suddenly his cell phone played a tune, disrupting her thoughts.

"I don't like you calling me unless it's an emergency," Chet said roughly into the phone.

Leah pretended to look out the window, stealing a glance or two out of the corner of her eye. Chet's normally relaxed posture had suddenly tensed. Bone white knuckles shone through the hand that clenched the tiny phone. His back straightened against the driver's seat. "Yes. All right. Look, I'll call you tonight. I have a beautiful woman by my side who requires my undivided attention." He paused. "Bingo, you got it. Now good-bye and don't call me. I'll call you."

Chet stuffed the phone into his suit-coat pocket. "Ol' brother doesn't know when to quit. He's unemployed like you were. He's been nagging me for a job."

"Is he a reporter?"

Chet laughed. "Not by a long shot. Washing windows is more his style. However, I only want to concentrate on getting you settled. You're worth every bit of my attention and more."

Leah sensed her fear that he expected a relationship had come true as they rolled into the parking lot of the *Gainsport Herald*. Her impressions were confirmed when Chet took her hand in his. "You'll do just fine," he whispered huskily in her ear before nibbling on her earlobe. She tried hard to bury her reservations while he led her into the office of the editor-in-chief of the *Gainsport Herald*. She noticed right away that the editor, S. Frank Haley, possessed a different personality than her ex-boss, Mr. Sanders. Day-old stubble covered his chin. Strange art decorated his walls, including a framed document of his divorce decree. When Haley caught her staring at the decree in puzzlement, a grin spread across his rugged face.

"The best thing that ever happened to me," he said, using a cigar from his shirt pocket as a pointer. "Freedom. Now it looks like I'll be making a move on wife number two."

"Really?" Chet said. "Congratulations. When's the big day?"

"We haven't made the decision yet." He lit the cigar. "After the fiasco with Delores, I sure don't want to make any more mistakes. Thank goodness there aren't any kids. Can you imagine her hounding me for child support? She'd be screaming at me worse than what I had to deal with in our marriage, or my torture chamber, I should say."

Leah fidgeted in her seat and twisted the strap of her purse. The smoke from the cigar stung her nostrils, prompting tears in her eyes. A ripple of pain from a developing headache taunted her temples.

Haley fixed his gaze on her. A small smile creased his dry

lips. Shirtsleeves were rolled up to the elbows, revealing hairy arms that rested across the desk. "Well now, Ms. Hamilton, Chet here says you're ready to come work for us. Glad to have you aboard."

"Y–yes, Sir."

"I want you to know that I run a tight office here. We're low-keyed, but that's because my workers give me what I want. You do your job and don't make waves; then we'll have a successful paper and a successful working relationship." He leaned back in his desk chair and puffed away on the cigar. "I'm sure you're quite eager to get started, Ms. Hamilton. Chet here covers major news stories for the paper and has expressed an interest in having you team up with him."

Leah cast a look at Chet to find his mouth curving upward into a small grin. "Sir, I would really like to—"

"Of course, there are plenty of other positions available in the departments; but since he feels you two will work well together, I would just as soon have you stay together and tackle the major stories. We have one brewing right now—a major corporation buy-out that looks like it will cost a bunch of jobs here in Gainsport. Since you're so good at interviewing, Ms. Hamilton, I'm instructing you and Chet to interview the two CEOs making the merger."

Leah gulped. "Well, Sir, I would just as soon work on something else. . .like personality profiles, for example. That's what I'm good at."

Haley took out his cigar and flicked the collection of ash into a tray. "I'll consider it. But for now, since this is a hot story, I'd like you to handle it with Chet. We'll see what you two can do; then I'll make my determination. Chet here has all the information you'll need to get started on the interview." He rose and shook her hand. "I must say, Ms. Hamilton, that Chet has good taste in coworkers. You certainly are a looker. I think you'll be quite an asset to our little paper."

Leah shriveled under his leering expression and hurried

out of the office. Once outside, she inhaled a sharp breath, thankful to have escaped the suffocating presence of Haley and the stench of the cigar that made her nauseous.

"That went great," Chet said with a smile. "So we're finally working together as a team. How I've longed for this day."

"This is not what I wanted," Leah said stiffly, following him to his office which was located in the opposite wing of the building. "I don't think it's a good idea for us to be working together. I'm used to working alone."

"The least you can do is keep a stiff upper lip and do this one project with me."

"I just don't know about any of this," she said dubiously, staring down the hall at the closed door of the editor's office. The inside of the place gave her the creeps, as did the editor-in-chief, who scanned her as if she were a hunk of meat hanging in the butcher's shop. For a moment she wished she were back in Mr. Sander's office, gazing at the pictures he displayed, including the framed verse found in the book of Proverbs.

She tried to push away her anxiety and followed Chet into his office. Stacks of papers occupied the corner of his desk and others overflowed from file drawers. Chet stuffed the papers into the steel drawers, indifferent to the crinkles he created, before switching on the laptop computer. Tapping the mouse control, he began leafing through the information he had already assimilated on the consolidation of the corporations. Leah sat beside him, staring at the information displayed on the screen, when a lone finger traced the curve of her arm. Breath, scented with morning coffee, fanned her ear. The sensation made her dizzy.

Leah stood and moved to the opposite side of the compact room. "I really think I should have my own office, don't you?"

"You're getting one tomorrow. You're too intoxicating. It's hard for a fellow to concentrate."

"Then why are we working together?"

"Because Haley is expecting great things from us. Like he says, if we do our job, things go much easier around here. He'll be in a better frame of mind to offer you another position, maybe even with the entertainment column and those personality profiles you enjoy so much. So let's go tackle this report."

The interview at the shipbuilding center proceeded without a hitch. Leah was amazed by Chet's smooth style during the interviewing process. He was concise in his questioning, nodding his head in the appropriate places and offering small comments when needed. Watching him in action, Leah couldn't imagine why Jim Richards would have been vexed by his technique. Chet gave the impression of a caring reporter looking to give an accurate portrayal of the news. His surprising manner made her reconsider for a moment the man she deemed as annoying as a mosquito.

"That was interesting," Leah said when they returned to the car. "You have the technique down to a tee. Jim was crazy not to give you an interview."

"So you wouldn't have thrown a book at me?"

"Not at all. I thought you handled the interview with professionalism. I guess. . .well, I guess maybe I've misjudged you these past few weeks."

Chet's eyebrows lifted. A slow smile spread across his face, accompanied by a glossy look in his eye.

"I thought you were overbearing, insensitive, and interested in your own self-preservation at the expense of everybody else. But you aren't that way at all."

"Leah, I really am a nice guy once you get to know me. I told you that first off during our initial date. I think you know now who the real creep is: Jim Richards. In fact, I think the cops should spend more time and resources investigating him as a possible suspect in the school shooting."

Leah whirled in her seat. "That's crazy. He had nothing to do with it."

"How do you know? You've seen how he is—mean, nasty as a snake, out to make everyone else miserable. Just remember, I've tasted his violent tendencies firsthand."

"You don't seriously think Jim could be involved? I mean, it's obvious he was at that computer show during the whole incident."

"Hello?" Chet knocked gently on her forehead. "Ever hear of the old-fashioned gangster who sends the boys out to do his dirty work? Richards is classic. These guys display the good-boy image on the outside, but on the inside, they're killers at heart. Don't you remember that incident when a man hired a guy to take out his wife in Chicago? Sure they seem like nice husbands and dutiful fathers on the outside, but the inside is a different story. Richards has the same personality trait. I don't think anyone has even considered investigating him more thoroughly. That's why this whole case has stalled."

Leah sat still in her seat, staring unblinking until her eyes began to hurt. The mere thought that Jim could do such a horrendous thing went beyond her sense of reasoning, especially after her conversation with Claire. "I–I don't know, Chet. That's a pretty ugly allegation, with little to go on other than being ticked at having a book thrown at you."

Chet started the engine. "At any rate, now you see why I don't want you involved with Jim or this whole fiasco. From now on, avoid Jim and Claire. For all we know, they could be a modern-day Bonnie and Clyde who have duped law enforcement and made everyone feel sorry for them."

Leah sat numb the entire way to the office. Doubts began to plague her.

That night, she sat in her usual spot on her sofa, contemplating Chet's words. Could Jim have done such a terrible thing? Could his depression have been triggered by deep-seated feelings of guilt for his involvement? Was all this religious talk of Claire's simply a cover-up for something more diabolical? Leah shivered at the thought. She took up a sofa pillow and encircled it with her arms, pressing it tightly to her, trying to calm the nervous trembling. Despite it all, the implications only renewed her interest.

❧

For the next few evenings Leah scanned reports on the case, searching for anything that might clue her in to a possible link with Jim and the murder of his wife. Suddenly the cell phone rang. With her eyes focused on the monitor before her, she answered the call. "Hello?"

"Ms. Hamilton?"

"Yes?"

There was silence for several seconds. Leah put down the papers. Every nerve stood at attention.

"This is. . .uh, Jim Richards."

In an instance, she felt her flesh turn to ice. Goosebumps broke out. Her fingers tightened around the tiny phone. She tried to greet him but found herself unable to respond.

"I hope you don't mind me calling you on your cell phone. Claire had the number."

Leah didn't remember giving Claire her number, but then again, she couldn't remember much these days.

"Look, I was wondering. . .I know this may sound crazy; but I'd like to meet with you over breakfast tomorrow, if that's all right."

Leah nearly dropped the phone on the floor. "Excuse me, is this really Jim Richards?" she said out loud, nearly kicking herself for asking such a ridiculous question. Yet the mere fact that he was calling seemed like a dream one might conjure up while working on a mundane project.

The voice hesitated. "I know it sounds impossible, but it is. Could you. . .I mean, would you consider it? I kind of owe it to you."

You owe me breakfast? Her neck broke out in a cold sweat. "Uh, you don't owe me. . . ."

"If you don't want to meet me, I understand. I just think,

well, I know I need to apologize big time."

Leah felt a dizzy sensation overtake her. "I have to be at the office by eight, but we could meet at six-thirty."

"The office? You found work? The last I heard you had. . ." He paused.

"Yes, I work for. . .uh, for another company outside of town. A friend found me a job." She didn't want him knowing that she worked for another newspaper, fearing the fact might ignite further hostility.

"So you don't mind meeting me?"

"That's fine. Where?" She scribbled down the address he supplied. "All right, six-thirty." After he hung up, Leah stared at her cell phone for the longest time, as if it had played some mean trick. "This is unbelievable," she murmured, clicking it off, "but maybe it's a blessing in disguise. Maybe now I can start filling in the empty spaces of this puzzle." In an afterthought, she picked up the cell phone again and called Chet with news of the abrupt invitation.

"You are not to meet with that man under any circumstances," came his harsh reply.

Leah sat back in her seat, startled by his tone of voice. "But don't you think this is a good thing, Chet? I mean, he asked me out of his own accord. Maybe I can do a little probing into what you alluded to the other day—you know, about him being a suspect."

"Are you crazy, Leah? That's precisely why I don't want you near him. He's a basket case. For all you know, he could be a serial killer, and you're next on his list of victims."

The threat sent shivers racing down her spine. "Chet, stop it. You're scaring me."

"I mean it, Leah. You're not to meet him."

"Look, there's no way this guy was involved. I think I'm a big enough girl to handle this."

"I'd rather you leave this up to me. I'll initiate an investigative probe myself. If Richards wants another interview, then

I'll be the one to conduct it."

"Sure, and we all know how much you loved the last interview. I've heard at least a dozen times about how he threw a book at you."

"So you'd rather he threw one at you? Or maybe you'd prefer something worse?"

"You're crazy! I can't take this. I just thought you would be interested in hearing what's happening, but I guess not." She hung up and fell back on the sofa. Chet was being totally unreasonable. How could she refuse this opportunity? This was the first glimmer of hope since she began a probe into the shooting. No matter what, she must go along with her instincts in this game and hope it would not lead her into danger.

ten

Jim sat in a corner booth of the diner, examining the selections depicted on the plastic-coated menu. Occasionally, he glanced up at the clock on the far wall above the counter. Customers on swivel stools chatted with the waitresses who refilled their mugs with steaming coffee. Already the coffee in his mug had grown cold from the long wait. He thought of ordering himself the special—a cheese omelet with toast—to settle the empty feeling inside his stomach, but instead vowed to wait. Surely Leah Hamilton would not miss this opportunity to meet. She had tried every trick in the book to meet with him before. Again, he glanced at the clock. *Seven o'clock. Half an hour late*. He sighed. *Where was she?* It seemed unbelievable to him that she wouldn't show up.

He turned the mug of coffee around in the circle. For the fifth time, the waitress came by and asked if he was ready to order the Wednesday special or have his coffee warmed. Jim shook his head and strained to see the people strolling outside the large plate-glass windows of the diner, scanning for Leah among the workers headed for their jobs. Would she really stand him up, perhaps as payback for the pain he had caused her? His fingers began to rap on the table. Another fifteen minutes came and went, with no sign of the pretty, long-legged reporter, wearing her classy suit and high heels.

At seven-thirty, a full hour after they were supposed to meet, Jim reluctantly dropped a small tip on the table and walked outside into the bright sunshine. He should have known this would happen. He paced down the street, angry with himself for trying to remedy a hopeless situation.

Pausing at the curb to await the traffic signal, he suddenly heard a "pssst" from a car parked at the corner. A young woman, adorned in dark sunglasses and a printed scarf, peered up at him. Jim stared for a minute, puzzled, then turned to head off across the street when a soft voice stopped him short.

"Mr. Richards, I'm Leah Hamilton."

He whirled.

"Please, get into the car." Leah opened the door. He promptly slid into the passenger seat.

"I don't understand." Jim stared at the sunglasses and scarf that covered her fine hair. "What's going on?"

"It's hard to explain." She engaged the engine.

"Where are we going?"

"Some place other than Main Street." She sped out into the traffic and drove for a time until they reached a country café. She pulled in and parked the car. "Sorry I had to do that. I hope you don't mind if we order a late breakfast."

"I didn't think you were coming."

"I was told not to, but I can make up my own mind."

Jim crinkled his brow in confusion as they got out of the car and headed into the café. A waitress promptly showed them to a small table where they sat down and ordered coffee. "I don't understand. Who told you not to come?"

"It's better I not say."

She slowly removed the sunglasses. Long, curly lashes blinked in his direction, framed by dark eyebrows arched in an inquisitive manner. Her high cheekbones, delicately curved nose, and red-tinted lips ignited sparks within him. A quick glance at her hand showed it devoid of a wedding ring.

"For awhile there, I didn't think you were ever coming out of that diner," Leah said with a smile. "You waited a long time for me to show up."

"A promise is a promise." He gazed up at the waitress who came with their coffee and ordered toast. Leah ordered a bagel with cream cheese.

"So what did you want to see me about?"

Abrupt and to the point. A reporter at heart. He dismissed the thought. "I–I just wanted to say that. . .that. . ." He saw the flowers in a box decorating the café window. "I've been watering the flowers you planted." He noticed her features soften. Dark brown eyes sparkled.

Jim fingered the mug before taking a sip. Leah sat tall, her head erect, gazing at her surroundings as if on the lookout for something of interest. Jim took it as a sign of a reporter on duty. "Like I said on the phone, I owe you a big apology. After thinking through everything, I let my feelings get in the way. I realize now you tried several times to ask for my forgiveness. I–I didn't want to let go." He stared at the plate of toast placed before him. "Honestly, you treated me well in that article you wrote. I read it again last night, every word." He gazed at her and watched the dark brown eyes mist over, like fog rolling across the landscape. "You didn't take any cheap shots when you wrote it, but displayed a real sensitivity that other reporters lacked in the whole situation. I was just too stubborn to see it." He inhaled. "I hope you will forgive me."

Leah stared at him with wide eyes, as if trying to analyze his intent.

"I overreacted big time, you see. I wanted others to feel my pain, and it wasn't right."

"You've been through quite a bit," she said softly, yet with a hesitation in her voice. "It can't be easy, especially when. . ." she hesitated, "the person who did this terrible crime is still on the loose somewhere."

"That's the worst part of all. I'd love to take out my hatred on that worthless piece of trash, whoever he is. I'd love to ask him if it made him feel like a man to shoot and kill a defenseless, pregnant woman."

They sat in silence. Leah picked up her bagel and took a few bites before stealing a glance at her watch. "Uh, look, I really need to get on to work. It's not wise to be late when you've just started a new position." She opened her purse.

"I'll take care of the bill. Thanks for meeting me. And I was wondering, would you care to take a walk in the park later tonight?"

Once more, the dark eyes perused him as if plagued by questions over his sincerity. Leah offered a small smile and a nod. "Make it tomorrow night. I may need to work late. What time?"

"Seven."

"Seven, tomorrow night," she said with a smile that made his heart perform somersaults.

❧

"This is unbelievable," she said to herself. "I just had breakfast with Jim, then he asks me to go for a walk. What's happening between us? Do I dare let it go on? What if Chet's assumptions turn out to be true? What if Jim is actually some deranged man, and I'm his next victim?" She shivered at the thought and shut her eyes momentarily, opening them in time to brake the car at a stoplight. "Jim wouldn't do anything of the sort," she reassured herself. "He was genuine today at the café. He talked about his wife's killer like someone seeking justice." She shook her head. "Chet must be off his rocker about this whole thing. He's been acting weird about all this from the get-go. Maybe that near miss with the coffee-table book shook up his brain too." The mere notion made her chuckle.

When she arrived at the newspaper office, Chet met her with a strange expression on his face. "Where have you been?" he barked. "You're an hour late."

"I had an errand to run," she said coolly. "I didn't know you were my timekeeper."

"You went and saw Richards, didn't you? After you promised me you wouldn't."

"I didn't promise you anything. I didn't see any harm in speaking to him for a few minutes. All he wanted to do was apologize for the way he's been treating me. I thought that was very nice of him."

"Well, you're in way over your head now. And the boss wants to see you."

"Huh?"

"Right now, little lady."

Startled and even a bit frightened, Leah followed Chet into the office where the boss sat in his chair, puffing on a cigar.

"Pull up a chair, Ms. Hamilton, and have a seat."

Leah did so. Chet slipped into a chair beside her. His face was grim, without the usual smile and confidence she had so readily seen in days past. Leah summoned up the courage to ask, "Is there something wrong, Sir?"

"Chet has brought it to my attention that you seem a little preoccupied lately." Haley struck a match and lit the huge stogie protruding from his mouth.

"I believe I've done my work, Sir. Perhaps he means that I'm not happy with my current assignment. You see, I. . ."

"Ms. Hamilton, I'm the one who assigns the responsibilities. I put you with Chet so you could understand our operations and how we do business. Now I find that you've been late to work and turning in less-than-adequate news stories. I'd like to know why."

Leah glanced at Chet out of the corner of her eye. He

stared straight ahead with his fingers tapping slowly on the armrest.

"We gave you this job under the assumption that you would follow the rules," Haley continued. "Number One rule is, I am the boss. Number Two rule is, you are the subordinate and are therefore to follow each and every assignment I give to you without question. Number Three rule is punctuality. I do not tolerate laziness or tardiness. Number Four rule—you are to keep yourself focused entirely on the assignments I give. I don't wish to hear you're involved with other assignments outside the jurisdiction of this office, or following news stories on your own whenever it suits you. It goes against my protocol and severely disrupts the flow of work that needs to be coming out of this office." He glared at her over his reading glasses. "You do need this job, Ms. Hamilton, don't you?"

"Yes, Sir, and I will try to—"

"Good. Then from now on, I expect you to fulfill your obligations. If I hear of any more difficulties, I'm afraid you will have to be terminated. And if that is the case, it's for certain that two terminations from two newspapers would not bode well for future employment. Am I clear, Ms. Hamilton?"

"Yes, Sir." Leah stood. "Is that all?"

Haley nodded before plugging the cigar back into his mouth. Leah turned and left, pausing outside to catch her breath. As she did, she could hear Chet and Haley conversing behind closed doors.

"So she's still interested in hanging around with Richards," came Haley's voice. "This has got to stop, Chet. I mean it."

"I've warned her, Frank, but—"

"She'd better reconsider her stand at this point. The man will soon be charged by the authorities anyway. . . ."

Several coworkers came down the hallway. Leah quickly stepped away from the door and opened her purse, pretending to rifle through the contents. When she turned, the door to Haley's office opened.

"Glad it's going to work out," Chet was saying. He closed the door, only to stop short when he saw Leah. "Are you waiting for me? Wonderful!"

"I'm waiting to find out why you and Mr. Haley are ganging up on me. I don't think I deserve it."

Chet frowned. "I know you don't believe me, but this is the truth. You're setting yourself up for a big fall if you continue the way you are, Leah. I don't want to see you hurt."

"Seems to me you're the one doing the hurting," she retorted, "like getting me in hot water." She whirled on her heel and marched down the hall toward her office.

Chet was beside her, stride for stride. "I'm only doing this for your sake. I wish I could make you understand. Some major developments are about to happen and. . ."

"Like having Jim arrested for a crime he had no involvement with?"

Chet grabbed her arm, stopping her short. "How did you hear about that?"

"I can tell you for a fact that it's not true. Jim had nothing whatsoever to do with his wife's murder. The very idea is absurd."

"What makes you so certain? For all you know, Richards could be a modern-day Dr. Jekyll and Mr. Hyde. He could have split personalities. Nice Jim and killer Jim, who turns on and off like a switch."

Leah shook off his hand. "You're crazy, Chet. Anyway, I have work to do."

Chet's fingers coiled around her wrist and pulled her into a vacant office where he shut the door. Anger creased his face.

His tie lay undone around the open collar of his shirt, revealing a crimson neck. "You're asking for trouble, you know that?" he hissed. "People are getting a little tired of you sticking your pretty little nose where it isn't wanted. You keep putting yourself in the middle of all this, and you'll wish you'd never written one word about the Taylor School shooting."

Leah pulled her arm out of his clenched fist. "Chet, what are you talking about? You aren't making any sense."

"I'm telling you to stay away from Richards. Leah, I love you. I don't want to see you hurt. That's all." He tried to bring her close.

Leah struggled out of his embrace. "I can take care of myself, thank you."

"The whole reason I got you this job was to keep you away from anything that breathed of school shootings. Crazy people are running around out there. . .people like Jim Richards. I don't want to see you duped by some madman."

"Maybe you're the madman by the way you're overreacting. Did you ever consider that?"

Chet trembled. "I'm warning you, if you care at all for our relationship or me, you'll stay out of this whole thing. If not, then we'd better call it quits right now." He stalked out, slamming the door behind him.

❧

Leah's anxiety over the day's events soon turned into a full-blown headache. When the workday ended, instead of returning home to nurse her headache, she drove to Elderberry Lane. Inside Jim's house, a lone light glimmered from a downstairs window. She sat in her car, pondering the idea of Jim doing anything to hurt his wife. . .or her, for that matter. Next door, she saw the lights on in the Hansons' house. Instinctively, Leah got out of the car and headed for the home, hoping the elderly Mrs. Hanson would remember her and provide some further insight into Jim's life.

"Why, if it isn't the young lady who planted the flowers!" Mrs. Hanson exclaimed when she opened the door.

Leah managed a small smile. "I'm sorry to be calling at this time of night, but—"

"Come right in."

"Who is it, Emma?" yelled an older man.

"The sweet girl who planted the flowers in Jim's yard, Herb," she replied. "And you never did tell me your name."

"Leah," she said quickly.

"What a pretty name. Come on in. We love meeting friends of Jim's." She ushered Leah into the living room.

Herb Hanson sat in a large recliner facing the television that spouted the evening news. A pipe dangled out of the crook of his mouth. He came to his feet and shook her hand. "Glad to finally meet you. Yep, you shore are a nice-looking gal. Emma kept talking about a nice-looking young gal who had planted flowers in Jim's front yard. Mighty kind of you to do that."

"So tell me, are you married?" Mrs. Hanson asked, out of the blue. "I think you and Jim would make a nice couple. I told him he should find himself a young lady. He's so lonely and miserable. You are friends, after all."

Leah balked. She felt her face flush. "I'm not married, but I hardly think that Jim and I are suitable—"

"You're not?" she interrupted. A broad smile filled her face. "Well then, come right in, sit down, and let me tell you all about Jim."

"But I. . ." Leah couldn't believe what she was hearing. For the next half hour, the older couple bubbled over with good things about Jim. Leah could tell they thought the world of him. He seemed like a son to them in many respects.

Leah sipped on the cup of tea Mrs. Hanson fixed for her

before placing it on the stand. "I do have a question for you. Is there any reason to think. . .I mean, were Kathy and Jim happy together? Living next door to them, did you ever hear arguing or anything strange going on?"

Mrs. Hanson glanced at her husband. "Not at all. They were the happiest couple I'd seen in a long time. They were always hugging each other, even out in the front yard." She giggled. "And yes, they smooched too. Quite a bit, as a matter of fact."

"I told Emma not to be spying on the neighbors," Mr. Hanson said gruffly. "She does what she pleases."

"I wasn't spying, Herb. I was just curious. It's good to see a young couple in love, with so many divorces happening nowadays. I'm happy to say that we've been married fifty-one years."

"That's wonderful."

"Yes. Anyway, Jim and Kathy were very happy. Jim was simply devastated over her death. He was here the other night, you know, all alone, simply miserable. I don't think he'd eaten in days. He had three pieces of the strawberry rhubarb pie that I made. Claire does come over nearly every day with his dinner, but I haven't seen much of her lately." Suddenly she straightened in her chair. "Oh, I just had the most wonderful idea! How about I have you and Jim over for dinner?"

Leah jumped in her seat, her elbow nearly knocking over her cup of tea. "Mrs. Hanson, I. . ."

"You are a friend of his, aren't you? That's what you told me."

"You see, I. . .uh. . ."

"Then you must come. I'll invite Jim, and we'll have a nice dinner, just the four of us. What do you think, Herb?"

"I think you're rushing things, Emma," he answered, "but

there's no sense in trying to talk you out of it. Once you've made up your mind, that's it." He turned to Leah. "You might as well give in, young lady. You won't change her mind."

"He calls me a busybody," Mrs. Hanson said with a laugh, "but I know people. You two are meant to be. Can you come Friday around six o'clock?"

"I–I guess so. Friday at six." Leah thanked the older couple for their time before drifting out of the house. A walk with Jim tomorrow. Dinner the following night. What was going on? She lifted her head to the skies and saw the twinkling stars. "Are You in on this too, God?"

eleven

Jim was at the park, right at seven as he promised. Before Leah revealed herself in the diminishing twilight, she watched him for a time. He paced in front of a bench with his hands in his pockets. Every so often he would lift his head to gaze at the trees swaying gently in the evening breeze. He then walked to the shore where the park nestled beside a flowing river, picked up some smooth stones, and practiced skipping them, one by one. They leapt across the water as if they had minds of their own. The scene brought a smile to her face as she thought of her early years, of long walks with her parents at the cabin by the lake, Dad teaching her to skip stones in the water, and rowing a boat out into the middle of the lake in search of new discoveries. The memories soon brought out the deep, dark clouds as well, hiding the peaceful images with confusion and despair. How she needed that peace in her heart. Jim and she were alike in many ways—each bound by tragedy and searching for a solution.

At last Leah came out of hiding and ventured up to the shore where Jim stood. The air was fragrant with honeysuckle blossoms growing around the trees that framed the river. "Hi."

Her voice made him whirl around in a start. He dumped the stones and wiped off his hands. "Hey."

"So, you like skipping stones? Dad taught me how when I was little."

"It takes practice," he admitted. "So, how are you?"

"Busy," Leah said with a sigh, dropping down on a bench.

Jim occupied the other end, keeping a safe distance between

them. "I see you're now working for the *Gainsport Herald*. I saw the article you wrote in the paper on the newsstand the other day."

Her face colored at the mention of the *Herald* and her days of reporting. *Not a pleasant way to begin*, in her opinion. "It wasn't my idea," Leah said hurriedly. "I was kind of desperate at the time. I'm considering leaving the job, anyway. It's just not for me. The editor, if you don't mind me saying, is kind of a sleaze."

Jim's eyebrows lowered in concern. "Then you should leave."

Leah jerked her head up, surprised by the tone of his voice and the concern expressed in his facial features. Why would Jim Richards care what happened to her? Not long ago, she was dubbed enemy number one in his book. Her hands began to shake. There was a change in him, but why?

"You can't stay in a place where the boss is like that," he went on. "And I wouldn't be caught dead working beside someone like Chet Frazier." He stirred in his seat. "That guy is no good. Did you know he once tried to pick up Claire? Thankfully, she's a strong Christian woman and could defend herself from the likes of him." He paused. "I'd stay away from him if I were you. He's trouble."

Leah opened her mouth to agree, but clamped it shut at the last moment. Despite Chet's brash behavior, he had seemed genuinely interested in her welfare. He had been there for her when there was no one else and arranged for the position at the *Herald* that saved her livelihood. Even with his headstrong personality, he had not taken advantage of their relationship. None of this pointed to a man prowling about, seeking her destruction.

"I won't tell you what to do," Jim continued. "If you think you should stay at the *Herald,* then do it. Only watch out for Chet."

"Honestly, I'm not that concerned about Chet. He's more conceited than anything. I just wish he hadn't been so nosy with you after the shooting last year. He really gave reporters a bad rap."

Jim shrugged. "It's to be expected. I know you all were only doing your job. I just wish everyone would stop pestering me and find out the person who did this thing. If the reporters could put all their efforts into finding the killer, rather than trying to find out what I'm doing, then maybe we would get somewhere."

"I know," Leah said softly. "I know exactly what you mean."

His turned to face her. "Do you really? Do you know how frustrating this has become? Look, I've known for a long time that the detectives were on a cold trail. No one seems to care about finding the killer this late in the game. And I've been too wrapped up in my problems to even think about looking for the animal myself."

Leah straightened. "I wish there was justice, but right now there seems to be none. Little girls have been murdered in their beds. Women are kidnapped and then left for dead in some farmer's field. The injustice in this world burns me to the core. I've been reading about the day of the shooting, Jim. Doing research on the computer. . .getting facts straightened out. I even ran into a policeman a few weeks back who was there at the scene. I haven't done much yet in trying to put the pieces of this puzzle together, but maybe I should. I don't know what will come of it, but perhaps I can be like those kids in Texas who used their heads and nabbed a killer. I've heard it said that everyone makes mistakes, and this killer has too. We just have to find out what it is."

The sudden silence proved deafening until a sniff sent Leah's gaze darting to a slow tear trickling out of Jim's eye. She promptly fetched a crumpled tissue from her purse.

"Thanks," Jim said, blowing his nose. "All I can say is, I

can't believe how I misjudged you, Leah. I thought you were like everyone else—looking for ways to get ahead in life and using other people's pain to do it. But y–you want to do the extraordinary and actually help. It's pretty amazing."

"It's not all that amazing," she said, her voice softening under the recollection of memories she had kept hidden away for so long. "It's something that's been brewing inside me. . . something I've been wrestling with for a long time. In fact, it hasn't even come to the surface until now."

The expression of concern that enveloped Jim's face forced Leah to focus her gaze on a patch of orange tiger lilies blooming nearby, made all the more brilliant by the setting sun. She inhaled deeply, and suddenly, the memories of long ago spilled out. "My family suffered a loss too. It happened when I was ten. My sister drowned in a pool. A baby-sitter was supposed to be looking out for the both of us. She let little Sophie wander out to the pool. The next thing we knew, she was floating belly down and not breathing. I remember screaming my head off at Alice to do something. She just stood there. All those precious minutes ticked by when Sophie might have been saved by CPR or something. My parents pressed charges of negligence against Alice. It went to trial, and the jury convicted her, but because Alice put on such a display for the judge, he let her go with probation and community service." A tear drifted down her cheek. "My sister is dead, and the baby-sitter got a slap on the hand. And I know what she was doing that day. . .talking to her boyfriend on the phone instead of caring for us. That's all she ever did when she came to baby-sit—talked on the phone and painted her nails. I tried to tell people, but they wouldn't listen. Nobody would listen. I was 'too little to understand,' they all said. But that girl's selfishness killed my sister. There was no justice at all."

"Leah," Jim murmured softly. He scooted across the bench. His hand came to rest on her arm. "I totally understand."

Leah swiped another tissue from the package inside her purse and blew her nose. "I've never told anyone this," she confessed. Glancing at the tissue in his hand, then looking at the one in her own, Leah began laughing. The noise interrupted the tense moment. "Look at us, Jim. Blowing our noses together while we share in the pain."

He cracked a faint smile. "It was meant to be. Both of us have carried the pain for so long. I've had it for just a year, but you've carried it for years."

"Fifteen years to be exact," Leah said. "Fifteen awful years. Fifteen years of watching my parents disintegrate into nothingness because of Sophie's death. Fifteen years of watching them grieve for her while I was left to cope with it on my own. I felt so lonely."

"I also know what it's like to be alone. Many years ago my parents were in a train derailment. They were in the passenger car and. . .well, you get the picture. They went to sleep, and I guess you could say, never woke up. After their deaths in the train accident, there was just Claire and me."

"Jim, I'm so sorry!"

He shrugged. "At least I know what happened to them. The train tried to avoid hitting a truck that had run the warning lights. It was an accident. Accidents are hard, but they are easier to swallow than a senseless murder."

"I–I suppose. I don't know. I've never been through something like the murder of a loved one. Sophie's death was probably the closest thing, and I was very young when it happened." Leah inhaled. "I guess we have a few things in common, don't we?"

"A few," he said with a smile.

Leah felt as though a lead weight had somehow been lifted from her shoulders—one she never knew had burdened her until the words came forth. "Anyway, now you know why I can't let go of this. I always thought perhaps I should go into detective work, but I love writing. Maybe, somehow, the two can come together." She hesitated, thinking once again of Chet's accusations. "We've got to get to the crux of this thing, Jim. You know, there are people accusing you of being involved in the incident."

Jim's face blanched at the news. He nearly fell over on the bench. "What? You–you can't be serious. Who is saying this?"

"I can't say right now, Jim, but rumors are floating around."

He brushed a hand across his face. "This can't be happening. Leah. . ." His voice trailed away. "Leah, you don't think that I could have. . ."

"No, of course not. But others do. Jim, the only way we can put the allegations to rest is to do some probing into this ourselves."

"You mean find out on our own, when the investigators have run into dead ends?"

"I know it sounds impossible, but maybe there's something that the authorities have overlooked. Other people have solved crimes. It isn't so farfetched. We have a killer walking the streets who thinks he's outwitted every law-enforcement officer out there. It burns me to the core. I think sometimes the real detectives in this world can be the ordinary Jim or Jane who lives in the suburbs. If there's any way I can do it, then I hope God will help me and maybe, just maybe, both Kathy's soul and yours can find rest."

"Leah, please, you have to believe me that. . .I loved Kathy, and I would never, ever—" He began to choke.

"Jim, I know." She brushed his broad shoulders, enjoying the strength of his muscular frame beneath the short-sleeved polo he wore. The color combination of his deep mahogany shirt and black pants proved appealing. "We're going to find out who's responsible, somehow, someway."

When they parted that night, Leah felt the bond with Jim had deepened beyond her wildest expectations. Not only was she committed to finding out who had done the deed, but she had also confided in him of her innermost secret. What was happening to her? Could the God that Claire believed in so strongly somehow be at work, trying to heal hearts torn by injustice? Or was she starting to fall in love with Jim Richards?

❧

The next day, instead of writing up an article requested by Chet, Leah concentrated on the promise she had made to Jim. It distressed her no end that Mr. Haley, Chet, and others thought to implicate Jim in the crime. She must lay it all to rest once and for all. After awhile, she reached into her pocket for her cell phone and dialed the Bakersville Police Department.

"Yes, I remember you, Ms. Hamilton," said Officer Clark. "Good thing you caught me. I'm here doing paperwork for a bit."

"Maybe I should call back another time."

"I'll be back out on the beat soon. What can I do for you?"

"You mentioned you were the initial officer at the scene of the Taylor School shooting. Is that correct?"

"Yes, Ma'am. A terrible day."

"Yes. The reason I'm calling is to. . .well, I'm looking to write up some kind of profile on the killer in the hopes it might generate public interest in finding the person or persons responsible. Are there any leads in the case so far?"

The chair squeaked, accompanied by an audible grunt. "I'm not at liberty to comment on an ongoing investigation by the homicide division. I can say that after a year, the trail sometimes gets cold. Detectives are still working on leads that are trickling into the office."

Leah inhaled. "I know this may sound strange, but after the events in Chicago with the deranged husband who killed his family, is there a possibility that Mr. Richards could be a suspect?"

"Ma'am, we ruled that out long ago. There were plenty of witnesses at the computer show who saw Mr. Richards giving a presentation at the exact time of the shooting. Of course, we did look into the possibility of a hit man, that sort of thing, but there was no proof that Mr. Richards wanted his wife murdered. I mean, there wasn't a struggle over money like an inheritance or insurance policy. There were no reports of domestic violence. Neighbors say they were very much in love. We know the victim, Kathy Richards, was pregnant at the time of her death; but from all accounts, Mr. Richards was looking forward to fatherhood."

"Why would a pregnancy give you reason to contemplate his involvement?"

"If you don't already know, it's a sick world we live in, Ms. Hamilton. Unfortunately, there are those who don't care to have offspring. They'll hire a professional hit man to do away with the mother so the kid isn't born. Sad, but true."

Leah swallowed the lump of distress that formed in her throat. Her stomach lurched. "That's horrible."

"A fact of life, no matter how rotten it is."

"So, are you still following other possible leads?"

"Yes, Ma'am, we sure are."

"And you can't give me any hints as to possible suspects? School kids? Irate teachers or former employees? A gangster?"

"I'm sorry. I can't comment on any possible suspects at this time. But I can safely say that the homicide division has ruled out family involvement."

Leah sighed. "At least it does give me some comfort knowing that Jim Richards is not a suspect. I didn't think it was possible, of course, but a coworker of mine was pretty insistent that he should be investigated, especially with the news coming out of Chicago."

"Unless we have proof, which of course we don't, since Mr. Richards was obviously out of town. The homicide division is now looking into other leads. Look, I only have a few minutes left before I need to get back to my beat. Is there anything else I can help you with?"

"Actually, I was wondering if you might meet me at the Taylor Elementary school yard—that is, if it wouldn't upset you too much."

A lengthy pause ensued. Finally, he said, "I'm not sure what that will prove, Ms. Hamilton."

"I'm not trying to prove anything. I just want to envision that day for myself, instead of making subjective observations over where everyone was and what they were doing. I would rather give the readers objective reporting. This is just a replay, you might say, given by someone who was there at the scene. Of course, if you prefer not to, I totally understand."

The pause made her wonder if she had made a mistake in asking.

"It's been a year since the incident," he said slowly. "I'll have to clear it with my boss. If he agrees, I could meet you around one P.M. this Saturday. I'm off this coming weekend."

Leah smiled. "Great. Thanks so much for your time, Officer Clark. I know I was lucky when you stopped me for speeding that day."

He chuckled. "I never heard of a speed trap giving someone a dose of luck. I suppose if it means coming in contact with someone who was involved at the scene of the crime, you would be right."

Leah clicked off the phone with an air of confidence, yet she knew this venture on Saturday would not be easy. She would be treading the same ground where the children's teacher had been so cruelly cut down, observing the tree where the madman had fired off the deadly round that stole a life, recreating in her mind the chaos that must have ensued. She clasped her hands together to steady her jitters. No, she had to do this. She had placed herself on a path of knowledge to solve this terrible crime. Remembering the faces of Claire and Jim, listening to the emotion in Jim's voice when he described his pain, and now the idea that others might be accusing him of the deed. . .these images drove her to find out anything she could about that day a year ago. Other reporters had been blessed with information that led to arrests. Perhaps she could uncover something so this might be put to rest once and for all.

twelve

Leah used the excuse of the dinner invitation at the Hansons' Friday night to hit the neighborhood mall and buy a new dress for the occasion. The dress might be a bit fancy for a casual dinner like this, but she wanted to make a good impression.

Chet had called several times in the interim, but she ignored his pleading voice over the answering machine. Life was complicated enough without embroiling herself in another confrontation with him. He would surely be irate if he were to find out about the Hansons' dinner plans and might even get her into more trouble with the boss. At the office, she kept herself busy with her assignments, refusing his offer for lunch out or conversation. Once he cornered her in her office and apologized for the day he grabbed her wrist and hauled her into a room for a tongue-lashing. Leah coolly accepted it before feigning the need to finish a piece. As far as she was concerned, their relationship was over.

Now brushing out her hair before the mirror, Leah wondered what this night would bring. Even if Mrs. Hanson thought of the dinner more like a matchmaking venture, Leah's investigative mind saw it as an opportunity for more information and possible leads. She would find out all she could about the people who once surrounded Jim and Kathy Richards, hoping to learn something in the process.

Leah arrived at the doorstep of the Hanson home, just as Jim emerged from his home and made his way across the lawn. He stopped short when he saw her at the door, then stepped back as if ready to return home. Instead, he took tentative steps forward until he paused on the sidewalk leading to the Hansons'.

"I'm surprised to see you here," he said.

"I was invited."

"You were? For an interview?"

"No, for dinner."

Jim scratched his head. "That's strange. I was invited for dinner too. Maybe Mrs. Hanson forgot that—" He began to chuckle. "No, she didn't forget. That sly little lady. I guess she thinks you and I should get together."

"I know. She told me. Listen, I don't mind playing along if you don't. I'd like to get to know the Hansons, anyway. They seem like a very nice couple."

Jim nodded. "They are. I owe them so much. They've become my adopted parents, so to speak."

"I could tell. Mrs. Hanson thinks the world of you. She's also very protective." Leah stretched out her finger, poised to ring the doorbell. "Shall we play along?"

"Sure. I've got nothing better to do tonight except stare at the walls."

The Hansons greeted them with open arms. Mrs. Hanson grabbed Jim in a hefty hold and gave him a kiss on the cheek. She stepped back to observe his crisp shirt and matching slacks. "You look very handsome, Jim. I haven't seen you dressed like that in so long."

Jim's cheeks turned a light shade of pink. "To be honest, I refused so many offers months ago, I haven't been invited anywhere for awhile."

"Well, come on in. Herb is just finishing the steaks on the grill." Leah and Jim entered the dining room to see the table set with Mrs. Hanson's expensive china and good silver. Once or twice, Leah stole a glance at Jim who kept his gaze fixed on the table. She wondered what was going through his mind, knowing the Hansons had invited them here for the purpose of bringing them together. She felt the warmth increase beneath her collar when Mrs. Hanson showed her a place opposite Jim.

"That's a lovely dress, Leah," Mrs. Hanson purred, "isn't it, Jim? I just love the lace around the collar and the midnight blue color. Very becoming."

Jim surveyed the dress for a long time. "Yes, it's very nice."

They sat down to a heaping platter of steaks, fresh corn on the cob, a large tossed salad, and dinner rolls. Leah immediately felt Jim examining her. She wondered what he was thinking.

"So, tell me how you two became friends," Mrs. Hanson inquired.

Leah choked on her glass of water. "Friends?" she sputtered. "Well. . .I. . ."

"You did tell me you were friends," Mrs. Hanson said, "while you were planting the flowers."

Leah stared down at her plate, suddenly realizing she had been caught in another falsehood. The dinner could only go downhill from here, as would her relationship with Jim, which had been going well up until this point.

"Leah came to my home for an interview awhile back," Jim interjected, with an ease that startled her. "You remember those stories in the *Gazette* about the anniversary of the shooting? Leah wrote those articles."

"Really? I had no idea."

Leah felt more like a cornered animal than an honored guest. She thought of feigning the stomach flu or other malady to excuse herself from what was sure to follow. Instead she tried another tactic. "I did interview Jim, but it was not by honest means. You see, I knew how much reporters had upset Jim in the past."

"We remember that too," Mrs. Hanson said, looking over at her husband. "It nearly drove poor Jim crazy. We finally had to tell some of those reporters to stop harassing him."

"That's reporters for you, always looking for the story. I thought I had the story and went over to his home, impersonating a friend to get an exclusive scoop on his life." She laid down her fork, conscious of the Hansons staring at her. "It was wrong. That's why I was there that afternoon planting flowers. I wanted to make amends. I only told you I was a friend so that you wouldn't get suspicious, finding me on his property."

"Despite her interviewing technique, she wrote a very good article," Jim continued. "Kathy would have been happy. I intend to mail a copy to her parents out in California. The article read like a diary. Leah captured our relationship better than anyone." He now stared directly at her. "She wrote with feeling. It wasn't just a news story. It was human."

"I'm very glad to hear everything turned out all right," said Mrs. Hanson, "but you know it's wrong to lie, young lady. I believe lying does more damage in this world than anything. It's better to face the truth."

"I found that out the hard way," Leah admitted. "I've decided I'm not really cut out to be a reporter. I think I should go back to my other line of work—writing personality profiles."

"You should stay with human interest stories," Jim interjected. "You can project the facts with emotion. You have talent."

Leah took her glass and quickly downed the water to dislodge the bit of salad caught in her throat. Jim was actually praising her abilities? A definite change had occurred within him. How it came about, she had no idea. At least she felt better that everything had been laid out in the open. They continued with their dinner, topped off by a triple-layer chocolate cake lovingly prepared by Mrs. Hanson. After some conversation, Leah rose to bid the couple good night. Jim left at the same time.

"Jim, I. . . ," she began as they strolled down the sidewalk.

He turned. "Yes?"

"Jim, I really appreciate what you said tonight, about my reporting and all. I know I've been really dishonest in the past."

"I meant every word. It took me a long time to see it. I'm just tired of being angry. I want to get over this and go on with life."

"Do you really think you can?"

"Maybe I could go on if I felt there might be justice in this whole thing. It seems like I'm caught in a vacuum. I can't go forward, and the past keeps sucking me back. I guess I need what everyone has been telling me: closure. The problem is, I don't know how to find it."

"Well, I'm meeting with the policeman I told you about at the park. We'll be at the Taylor Elementary playground tomorrow, where he's going to show me the crime scene. I'm hoping something he says will give me some clues. Do you want to come?"

Jim seemed shaken. He stared at the ground. "I can't go back to that place," he whispered.

"What?"

"I'm sorry, Leah, but I can't go there. To the playground, I mean. Too many memories. I. . ."

"Jim, it's okay. I just wanted you to know what's happening and what I'm doing."

"Leah, I do want to help. If there's any other way I could . . .believe me, I would. I don't want others thinking that I could have been involved." She could hear the words choking up in Jim's throat. He turned and began walking back to the house.

Leah followed him. "No one will, Jim. The police officer I spoke with said you are definitely not a suspect."

He paused, frozen on the sidewalk. "But that doesn't clear my name with others who have suspicions. Who knows what rumors are being spread? This can only get worse."

"It won't. I won't let it."

Jim turned to look at her. He then came toward her and stopped. He reached out tentatively toward her, unsure at first, then slowly traced a line across the curve of her cheek. His fingers swept one side of her face, then the other. Leah felt every nerve stand at attention. Her breath nearly left her at his touch.

"Leah, I. . . ," he began. The words became dammed up inside of him. "Good night." He turned and strode to his house. Leah touched her cheek before proceeding to her car. She thought about his words and his touch that electrified her. It seemed impossible to think that something wonderful might be happening between them, yet the attraction was there. She felt it at dinner, when he gazed at her from across the table, and again, even stronger, just moments ago. Leah pressed her lips together. Now she was more determined than ever to find the person who had hurt Jim. She needed a breakthrough to put that man behind bars.

At that moment, a thought trickled into her mind from the sermon at Claire's church. *With God, all things are possible.*

"Everything is possible with You, isn't it?" Leah said. "Oh, I hope so."

❧

Leah returned home that night to five messages waiting for her on the answering machine, all of them from Chet. She tapped her fingernails on the counter of the kitchen. She replayed his messages on the speaker, his sultry voice explaining how sorry he was for invading her life, and would she please call so he could apologize. The last message told her that he needed to speak to her about a newspaper piece.

"Chet, you're impossible," she whispered. Shrugging, Leah picked up the phone and dialed Chet's number. She heard several male voices conversing in the background when a stranger answered the phone.

"Hello, is Chet there?"

She waited, listening with interest as a man in the background attempted to hush his companions. Chairs scraped across a linoleum floor, followed by the sudden click of the radio. Jazz music drowned out the noise.

"Hello, Sweetheart!" came a familiar voice. "I've missed you. Where have you been?"

"What are you doing, having a party? And how did you know it was me?"

"A good guess. You might say I'm having a party. A few friends came over to play cards since I didn't have my favorite girl to go out with me tonight."

Leah bristled. "I'm very busy."

"Too busy that you can't keep up with old friends?"

"I thought we were through, Chet."

"Now, Leah, I was only kidding the other day. I got a little hot under the collar. Frank wants decent work from us, and he's been getting on my case. He still thinks you're too wrapped up in the school shooting incident and Jim Richards."

"Really, Chet, it isn't any of your business."

"Unfortunately, it is when the boss is barking at me about productivity. You heard the ultimatum."

"Yes, and I've been on time and delivering my work."

Chet's breathing fanned over the receiver. "Really. You were a day late on that piece I asked you to finish. You sure other things aren't occupying your mind again? Like Taylor Elementary, or even Jim Richards?"

"And if it is?"

"Leah. . .it's been spelled out backwards and forwards. You lose this job, and that's it for you. I don't want to see that happen, not after I got this job for you in the first place. It's my reputation on the line."

"Don't worry, I won't tarnish your reputation."

"Look, I can't stress enough that you not try to become Wonder Woman and nab the bad guys in this whole Taylor thing. Not only is it unrealistic, it's dangerous."

Leah wondered then if Chet knew about her conversation with the policeman, but how could he? She was alone at the time, and she had used her cell phone. He couldn't know. . . could he? "Like I've said in the past, I'm a big girl, Chet. And I already have a father."

Over the line, she could hear his teeth grating. "You just think about what I've said. You keep going the way you are, and soon you'll be in way over your pretty head."

I'm already in over my head, Leah thought, replacing the receiver. Her hand rested on her face where Jim had so lovingly caressed her with a sweep of his hand. *Sorry, Chet. Nothing you say is going to make me change my mind. Not now. . .not ever.*

thirteen

Jim noted the reaction on Claire's face when she brought over a chicken casserole for dinner, as if she could sense the change within him. Since his meetings with Leah, he found peace entering his soul for the first time in over a year. He welcomed the peace that provided a respite from the anger, grief, and loneliness he had wrestled with since Kathy's death. Claire's mouth dropped open in astonishment when he offered to take the milk-glass casserole from her hands and reheat it in the oven.

"Is your job going better?" Claire wondered.

"I've been working hard at it. I'm slowly picking up a few customers."

"Is there anything new to report?"

He shrugged. "Nothing from the police, if that's what you mean."

Claire continued to stand in the kitchen and stare while he opened the cupboards to remove plates that had not decorated the table since Kathy's demise. Paper plates and plastic cups had been the normal dinnerware. He even went to the chest of drawers in the dining room, opened it, and retrieved placemats and linen napkins.

"Jim, what's going on?"

"I'm just tired of living like a beggar." He turned to acknowledge he'd startled her. "And it's about time I thanked you for all you've done this past year. No brother could have a more caring sister."

"Oh, Jim!" Claire flung herself into his arms, her tears staining the collar of his shirt. "I don't know what's happened, but God has answered my prayers."

"I've still got a long way to go, but I–I've started by making amends with Leah."

Claire disengaged herself from his grasp. "You have?"

"We were invited over to the Hansons' for dinner by separate invitations. Obviously, the Hansons wanted to get us together. You could say the couple is looking out for our welfare. We both got things out that needed to be said."

Claire took up his hand and gave a squeeze. "Jim, that's great news!"

"I just hope Leah can really forgive me. I could kick myself for overreacting like I did about that interview."

"I'm sure Leah's forgiven you."

Jim twisted his lips and turned back to the table to place the dinner plates, sprinkled with blue cornflowers, on the placemats. "Maybe. She does seem to care. After rereading that article she wrote about Kathy and me, I could tell she really understood my heart. Not many people do."

"Leah is really a sensitive person. I can tell she was upset over what's happened to the both of us. It's hard for others to empathize with people after they go through such terrible things. They don't know what to say or how to react, but I think Leah has tried to understand. She wrote about your pain in such vivid description, I was deeply moved. It's rare to find reporters with that kind of style."

Jim nodded, thinking about Leah standing on the sidewalk of Elderberry Lane with her beautiful hair cascading over her shoulders. Her hair mesmerized him. Not many women these days wore their hair that long. The dark strands reflected the streetlights that night. And her skin—it felt soft like a rose petal. How he wished then that he had kissed her to see if her lips were equally as soft and tender. He shook his head and stooped to remove the steaming casserole from the oven. "This is enough to feed a small country," he observed with a chuckle.

"Why don't you put it back in the oven on low and see if Leah would like to join us?"

Jim stared at his sister with wide eyes. "You mean call her up, out of the blue?"

"Why not?"

"That's a good idea. Maybe you and she can talk more. I'd like her to know more about. . .well, about God. She needs to hear the message of the gospel. I don't know if she's a Christian."

"That's a good idea. She's been on my heart lately." Claire jumped to reach the phone and dialed the number. She stood still for several moments, left a message, then hung up. "She's not home right now."

"Well, we tried." Jim sighed, wondering if he would have the nerve next time to follow through with his inclinations. Just about everything in him shouted *Yes!* but a small voice whispered reservation deep within.

❧

Leah arrived at the school grounds ten minutes early for the meeting with Officer Clark. He had called her that morning, moving their meeting time to four o'clock. She came wearing a disguise, knowing that if Chet caught wind of her activity, it might mean the end of her career. Fingers adjusted the large sunglasses covering her eyes and the colorful kerchief wrapped around her head. The outfit of a ratty old shirt and dirty blue jeans lent her the appearance of some homeless person off the street. She hoped the officer would remember her, despite the strange apparel.

After an hour wait, a car pulled up, bearing the policeman clad in plain clothes. When Leah emerged from her vehicle, the man gave her a quizzical look.

"Are you. . . ?"

"Yes, I'm Leah Hamilton. I'm the one you caught speeding a few weeks ago, Officer Clark."

His face relaxed at the mention of the ticket. "I guess I won't ask why you're dressed like that."

"It's better you don't."

Clark heaved a sigh and sunk his hands into the pockets of his trousers. "I didn't want to come back here," he said slowly, focusing his gaze on the simple brick building resting on a small incline. The place appeared serene. Nothing spoke of the horror that had unfolded there a year ago but the small dogwood tree in the front of the building, decorated with a red ribbon. "That's the anniversary tree the school planted in honor of the teacher who was slain," he pointed out.

Leah followed the brawny man. His feet scuffed along the blacktop, his eyes squinting to the left side of the building and the new playground equipment in the distance. They both mounted a set of steps.

"This is where it all happened," Clark acknowledged, waving his hand at the playground. "I tied the yellow police tape around the crime scene. I can still hear the kids crying and the whine of the rescue vehicles." He shuffled forward, turned, and pointed. "Kathy Richards was lying right there in that spot."

Leah made some notations in a small pad she carried in her pocket.

Clark continued. "Yeah, it was tough. Can you believe an elementary playground turned into a murder site? It's a sick world sometimes, Ms. Hamilton."

Leah pulled her sunglasses down to the tip of her nose to survey the site. She tried to visualize that day, only to find the emotion swelling within her. She turned and traced the path behind the officer, watching as he pointed out where the person who did the deed hid that day.

"The killer sat in that tree over there."

Leah and the police officer climbed the hill behind the playground to the oak tree. The tree still bore a wound at the place where the branch had broken off. An indentation in the ground still marked the impact of the tree branch and perhaps the killer himself. Leah sucked in her breath. She cupped her hands around her eyes to block out the sun and observed the playground from the killer's vantage point. Scenes of that terrible day trickled through her mind. "Why would someone want to shoot off a gun into a playground full of children?"

"Why does anyone want to kill innocent people? They're crazy, psychotic, maybe even possessed. Some do it for the thrill, others for the publicity. In the case of school shootings, most of the kids want to see their handiwork plastered across the television screen or on the front page of newspapers. Others do it because they were treated unfairly by faculty and students."

"But this is an elementary school. Could the killer have been a previous student with a grievance against Kathy Richards, for example?"

"A revenge shooting? It's always possible. However, from what we've gathered in a profile on the deceased, Mrs. Richards was loved by everyone in the school."

"Was anyone else on duty at the playground during that time?"

"We know that a Mr. Ramirez was seen at the playground around the same time as the shooting."

"Mr. Ramirez?"

"He taught Spanish to the fifth graders. Some kind of special program to introduce a foreign language class to the younger kids. They were trying it out that year."

"Have you interviewed him?"

"Of course. We interviewed all witnesses to the shooting. He was pretty broken up about it all. Said he had come to give Kathy back a homework assignment. I guess she had been taking Spanish lessons on her lunch break. Said he wished he had died instead of her."

Leah again surveyed the scene and the tree where the killer huddled with his weapon clutched in his hands, waiting for the opportunity to open fire. Once more, she surveyed the playground. It seemed inconceivable that someone would open fire on a teacher without a motive. Then again, what kind of insanity would prompt such an action?

She began to choke from the emotion building up within. "I think I've seen enough. Thank you for taking the time to show me this, as hard as it's been for you." Tears blurred her eyes as Leah stumbled back to the car. Once inside, she threw off the sunglasses and untied the scarf that held back her long hair. Never in her life had she felt so distressed by a situation. Somewhere the killer roamed free, without the punishment he rightly deserved. The whole thing sickened her to the core.

Leah arrived at her apartment, her mind buzzing with information. For some reason, she couldn't get the Spanish teacher named Ramirez out of her head. She made a mental note to check the phonebook for all Ramirez listings and see if she might snag an interview with him. Just then she noticed a strange car sitting in a parking space near her apartment. A familiar voice stopped her in her tracks.

"Hi, Leah."

She spun around to see the driver's window roll down and a face poke out. To her surprise, Jim Richards stared at her through the open window.

"I brought you dinner," he said, patting a dish wrapped in a plaid cozy, sitting on the passenger seat. "That is, unless you've already eaten."

"Actually, I haven't."

"Then here." He handed the dish out the window into her startled hands. "It's a chicken casserole, prepared by Claire. I warmed it up for you."

"That's really nice of you. Thanks."

"Don't mention it." He started the motor. "Hope you like it. We were going to eat the casserole but decided we didn't feel like it."

The warmth of the casserole dish filled her hands and radiated down her arms until her whole body felt warm. "Would you be interested in sharing this? It looks like enough to feed a small army."

Jim chuckled. "That was my sentiment, except I compared the amount to a small country. Claire fixes a ton, even though I'm just one person. Sure, I'll join you."

He turned off the engine and got out of the car, dressed in tan Dockers and a polo shirt, stylish as always. Leah inhaled sharply as she led the way to the door. Jim Richards was actually coming into her apartment. It seemed more like a dream than reality. She fought to control the tremors of her hands.

"Here, I'll hold the dish while you open the door."

Leah flashed a small smile, hoping he would not notice the gold key shaking in her hand. Once inside, she took the dish and headed for the kitchen.

"Nice place," he commented, following her. She unwrapped the dish and set it on the table. "Have you always lived here?"

"Only a few months, when I took the job at the *Gazette.*" The mention of the ill-fated newspaper sent heat crawling into her cheeks. Why did she have to mention the paper that initiated all the trouble between them? She glanced over to size up his reaction to the blunder but found his face impassive while he scanned the journalism books lining a shelf. He then studied the herb planter and the tiny plants all in a row.

"So you've taken up gardening since planting the flowers at my place?"

"Well, as much as one can do in an apartment. Maybe one day I'll have my own house and a garden too." She bit her lip then at the thought of living in Jim's house. "I can't do that."

"Do what?"

"Oh, nothing. Just thinking." She sat down at the kitchen table. "I met with the police officer today at the school."

A muscle quivered in his jaw. "How did it go? Learn anything?"

"Maybe. There's something I need to ask you."

"I'll try to answer it if it's not too painful."

Leah whipped out her pad to study the notes she had taken. "Did your wife ever mention to you a Spanish teacher named Ramirez?"

"Ramirez?" Jim furrowed his forehead. "A couple times, I think. Kathy was taking Spanish lessons. I figured it was a kick she was on. Why?"

"Just wondering."

Jim sat upright in his chair. "Leah, if this has anything to do with Kathy, I have a right to know."

"It's probably nothing, just that the police officer I chatted with said Ramirez was probably a witness to the shooting. I'm wondering if Ramirez would know anything more, having been on the scene." She sunk her chin into her hand. "I doubt it, though. Surely the police have already interviewed him thoroughly. It's probably a dead end."

"It sounds like a good lead to me. I'll take anything at this point, anything at all."

The aroma of the casserole filled the apartment. Leah fetched plates and silverware. Jim sat quietly at the small dining table, staring directly at her. Leah straightened, bewildered by his expression, and began dishing up the casserole. "This looks great." When she turned to give him a plate, he was on his feet and at her side. His manly scent warmed her to the tips of her toes. Her hand began to tremble, tilting the plate sideways.

Jim rescued the plate before the contents spilled. "Leah, I just wanted to say that I really appreciate what you're trying to do. But please, don't get yourself in too deep."

"What? Why? I thought you wanted to find out who did this and—"

"I care about you very much." His tender hand came calling once again, this time around her shoulder. He rubbed the place with affection. "I–I never thought I would care about anyone, especially a reporter." He nearly laughed until his face became serious. "But I do care. I don't want to see you hurt because of me."

"Jim. . ." Before she could say anything, she felt the pressure of his lips on hers and his arms drawing her close. His hand slowly combed through her long hair. The kiss intensified until suddenly, he pulled away.

"Leah. . .I need to know something. Are you a Christian?"

"A Christian?" She paused. "I believe in God. I talk to Him sometimes."

"But have you made a commitment and accepted Jesus into your heart?"

Leah stared at him, suddenly bewildered by this questioning after such tender contact. "Well, I. . ."

Disappointment clearly overshadowed his face. He returned to the dinner table, sat down, and lifted his fork but did not eat.

"Jim, I don't understand. Why are you asking me this?"

"It's just something I've been thinking about. You see, I'm a Christian. According to the Bible, I'm not supposed to have a special relationship with anyone who isn't a Christian. Leah, I want you in my life. I think about you all the time. I can't continue like this unless. . ."

"Unless I'm a Christian?"

He nodded solemnly.

Leah didn't know what to think. She stared at the food on her plate, feeling the tender moment they had shared evaporate like water in the hot sun. They talked for a bit about their lives, but clearly their relationship had taken a sudden dive. When he left that night, Leah felt more confused than ever before. *God, are You there? What does Jim mean that we can't be together unless I'm a Christian? I don't know anything about it. Maybe I can try, for his sake, but wouldn't that mean becoming someone I'm not? And isn't that how I got into trouble in the first place?* She mulled it over until exhaustion won, and she fell asleep on the sofa.

fourteen

"¡Hola!. . .uh, do you teach Spanish? I mean español? I would like to learn your language and. . ."

Leah held the receiver away from her ear at the shouts of broken English. "Yes, I mean, sí, I understand. So no one there is a teacher. Sí, yes, thank you. . .gracias." She banged down the phone and penciled out another Ramirez on the list of ten generated by a quick scan of the phonebook. This man named Ramirez definitely intrigued her. When she called the elementary school and discovered that he had left his teaching post the day after the shooting, she became all the more curious. Surely Kathy's death could not have rattled him *that* much, unless he knew something. She scanned her list. Four Ramirezes were dead ends. One had an answering machine. She tried the sixth.

"La Casa Restaurante," came a thick voice.

"Oops, I must have the wrong number. I was trying to find a Mr. Ramirez."

"Mr. Ramirez? Señorita, there are four Señor Ramirezes here. Which one do you wish to speak with?"

"Oh. Do any of them tutor in Spanish? I hear that a Mr. Ramirez gives Spanish lessons in his free time."

There was a pause. Leah felt her heart skip a beat. "Miguel used to teach, but he is out of the country right now."

"Out of the country?"

"He went back home to Colombia."

"Really. I was hoping to hire a tutor. You see, I'm planning a trip to a Spanish-speaking country soon, and I wanted some lessons."

"Too bad. Miguel teach good."

"Has Miguel always taught Spanish?"

"Sí. He liked to teach the leetle cheeldren. He say they learn better than adults."

Leah's heart flipped. "Really. Hey, would you mind if I stopped by your restaurant to speak with you about Miguel?"

Again, a pause ensued.

"When he returns, I want to make sure I hire him as a tutor. I intend to pay well, you see. I have a small fortune to spend, if the tutoring is excellent. Like a hundred dollars a lesson?"

"Ah! For that, I teach you myself. Come by tomorrow and we talk."

"And where is your restaurant?" Leah jotted down the directions to the restaurant and the time. "Thank you so much. And your name?"

"Eduardo. Miguel's brother."

"Eduardo. Thanks again. I'll see you tomorrow morning." Leah replaced the phone with a smile. "I found him!" she said in glee. "Miguel must have been the teacher who was with Kathy the day of the shooting. A quick check of the school files will confirm it." She rubbed her upper lip. "Interesting, though, that he suddenly decides to jump ship and head back to Colombia, right after the shooting occurred. I wonder what really spooked him?"

The shrill of the phone startled her out of her contemplation. Even when Chet's smooth voice came over the line, Leah only smiled, too excited over her discovery to care that he was the caller.

"You sound like you're in a good mood. I take it that means you'll go out with me."

"What?" she asked absentmindedly.

"Tonight's the night, Leah. I can feel it. I need to tell you what's been in my heart. So, how about a candlelight dinner

. . .unless you still plan on hanging out with a loser like Jim Richards."

Leah tensed. For a second, she had the distinct impression that Chet knew everything about Jim and her—the dinner, the kiss, and Jim's ultimatum. But he couldn't know. . . . She shook her head. "How about La Casa Mexican Restaurant?"

Chet cleared his throat. She heard papers rattle. "Why do you want to eat there, of all places? Do you like Mexican food or something?"

"I've got a hankering for tacos all of a sudden." She began to chuckle.

"Sounds like it's more than that."

"Oh, nothing. Nothing at all. Just for once, things seem to be going a little my way. It's about time, too. Hey, maybe I'll take Spanish lessons. Do you speak Spanish, Chet?"

A cough came over the phone. "No. I have a hard enough time with the English language, and especially when someone is playing games with the English language. Really, Leah, you've told me how mature you are. So how about stopping with the games like eating tacos and learning Spanish."

"This isn't a game. You all think there isn't anything to this school shooting, that I'm some sort of wacko trying to solve things on my own. But I've got a good lead. I know it."

Chet's voice became strangely quiet as he said, "Really now. So, what lead is this? You found out Richards likes tacos?"

"No. For your information, I just found out that some guy named Ramirez was on duty the day Kathy was shot. Then the day after the shooting, he vanished. I called around until I found this restaurant that his family owns. His brother said he'd gone back to Colombia. Now why would he leave like that? The man must know something. I'm sure of it. Maybe his relatives at the restaurant know something too."

Chet's raw laughter sent a nervous chill racing up her spine. "Big deal. So Ramirez was spooked and didn't want to come back to school. I'd jump ship too, if I were in his shoes."

Leah's hand clenched the phone as the words rang in her ears. *Why would Chet say something like that? It's almost as if he knows more about this whole thing than he's letting on. If he's done his own investigative probe, why won't he clue me in?* "I suppose," she answered coolly, yet inwardly, her heart began beating like a player on a snare drum.

"So, to change the subject, I guess you're still not interested in dining with me."

"Sure I am, Chet," Leah said. She had nothing to lose at this point and perhaps everything to gain, especially if Chet knew something about Ramirez. "What time?" She could almost hear the grin filtering over the phone.

"Wow, great! And I thought this was a lost cause. Let's see. . . . I'll pick you up at nine. We'll make it a late dinner, under the stars."

She laid the phone down, but her mind buzzed with information. *I'd jump ship too, if I were in his shoes*. "Chet knows more than he's saying. I'm sure of it. A comment like that just doesn't zoom out without a reason. I'm going to find out tonight, right under those stars of his."

All at once, Leah grabbed her purse and headed for the car. She drove nonstop until she reached the empty playground of Taylor Elementary. She needed to return here as a refresher before dinner with Chet. A cold wind from the north gave her goosebumps. She stood in the midst of the empty playground. Evening shadows filtered across the lonely swing sets and abandoned slides. In the wind she could hear the gleeful shouts and songs of the children as they played. All at once, the cheerful sounds were broken by the sound of a loud pop, like a firecracker on the Fourth of July. Children's screams filled the air. A shadow collapsed on the ground. . . . The feeble voice of a young woman called out the name of her love as if she knew she would never see him again.

Leah walked over to the tree where the killer hid that terrible day. She turned and made a straight path toward the school. "This is what would have happened if the killer had a direct shot." She scanned the ground to the right of where Kathy Richards had fallen. Again she retraced her steps to the tree and the place where a heavy branch had broken off on the right side. "A broken tree branch. What if the branch the killer was sitting on broke while he was aiming? The gun went off as he fell. . . ." Leah paused.

She again thought about Chet's words—*I'd jump ship too, if I were in his shoes*. "You would jump ship if there's danger, like a ship about to sink. What if your ship was sinking? Ramirez was scared to death. . .not because of what happened to Kathy. . ." She glanced up at the tree. ". . .but what could have happened to him." Tremors seized her. *The killer must have accidentally shot Kathy instead of his intended target: Miguel Ramirez. It must be true. That's what happened! And when Ramirez saw what was going on, he ran for his life, right back to Colombia.* Leah inhaled several quick breaths, trying to steady her nervous jitters.

At that moment, she spotted a dark figure watching her from afar. She retreated as he approached, trying to will her feet to take flight. As he drew closer, his hand reached into the pocket of his jacket. Her feet finally responded. She took off for the woods as fast as her legs would allow.

"Leah, wait! It's me, Jim."

"Jim!" Leah nearly fell from the force of her sneakers skidding across the ground. "You scared me half to death!"

"I figured when you didn't answer your phone that you were here. Somehow, I knew." He slowly ventured to the playground and stood still with his hands tucked into the pockets of his jacket. A cloud of despair swept across his face. "This place is like a picture of hell for me; a reminder of death and destruction."

"What made you come?" Her voice shook from both the abrupt encounter and the cool of the evening.

"You. Since you seem so determined to find this guy, I thought the least I could do is help."

"Oh, Jim, you won't believe what I've discovered. Come with me, and I'll show you." She retraced her steps, telling him in detail the thoughts streaming through her mind. "I should go to Officer Clark with this information."

"They've been through it all, Leah," he said, shaking his head. "I'm sure they've already questioned this Mr. Ramirez."

"But now he's out of the country, like his brother said. It would be impossible to interview him further if he's in a violent nation like Colombia."

"You think he took off?"

"From someone trying to kill him, yes."

"So you're saying someone was trying to kill Ramirez and ended up killing Kathy instead?"

"Look at it from the killer's viewpoint. I know you don't want to, Jim, but it makes sense. The guy wasn't looking to hurt any kids, but he needed the commotion of the kids to cover his deed. He probably thought with all the school shootings recently, he would never be caught and the police would focus their attention on deranged kids as suspects, like in school shootings of the past. So he sat up in the tree, waiting for a clear shot at Ramirez. When the time came to make the hit, the killer was confident he could get the guy. Suddenly, the branch broke just as he fired. The bullet hit Kathy instead of his intended target: Miguel Ramirez. It wasn't supposed to happen that way. Scared and confused, he took off into those woods." She pointed at the forest glade beyond. "And somewhere, the deed is eating away at him like a cancer."

"I hope it is," Jim said bitterly. "I hope he can't eat or sleep. Anyone who tries to kill someone while there are innocent kids and a teacher playing in front of his gun is evil. If he didn't want to harm anyone else, why pick a time like that to do his deed? Why not wait 'til the guy walked out to his car or at his house?"

"We need to know why the killer wanted Ramirez dead in the first place. If we find that out, then maybe we'll know why he chose the playground as his cover. But I still believe the guy was not targeting anyone else but Ramirez."

"I don't know, Leah. It doesn't make sense. In a way it does, but in another way, it just looks like he was out for blood and sacrificed Kathy's life for a cheap thrill." Tears glazed Jim's eyes before he looked away.

"Oh, Jim," Leah crooned, gently touching him. "I'm so sorry for all the torment you've suffered. It isn't right, I know, but maybe with these breakthroughs, it will eventually lead us to the one who did it."

"Maybe," he said as they headed back to their respective cars. "But I'm not holding my breath. Life hasn't dealt me a fair hand so far. I'm not expecting any miracles now."

Leah turned with her hand on the handle of her car. "Jim, I spoke with some of Miguel's family members. They own a Mexican restaurant here in town."

Jim's eyes searched out hers above the roofs of their cars.

"Let's head over to that Mexican restaurant right now. I told that Eduardo guy I'd be by in the morning, but let's see if they will tell us something. We have to find out why someone would want to kill this Ramirez. That's the key."

"Okay, let's go."

She threw herself behind the wheel with nervous adrenaline soaring through her. "Lord, they have to tell me something. Please, give us a clue." She halted, suddenly realizing she was praying. At that moment she recalled the conversation she had with Claire about releasing one's burden to the Lord. A tremendous burden now weighed on her—the burdens of Kathy's death, Jim, Ramirez, and Chet all rolled into one. Intermixed with this was a certain fear that gnawed away at her strength. For so long she had lived life in her own strength. Now, as she grew closer to the answer, she felt the weight of fear bearing down on her. Fingers clenched the wheel as she turned into the crowded parking lot of the restaurant. Jim's car followed. "Lord, please help us," she murmured. "I–I know we can't do this without You."

Leah rose from the car to see the creases furrowing Jim's jaw and the fire in his eyes. "Jim, we have to be careful," she whispered to him. "We can't go storming in there. The only way we can get the information we need is to be tactful."

"Tactful," he repeated with a hardness in his voice that made Leah wary. "Look, if that guy you were speaking about knows who killed my wife, then I'll be the first to know."

"They told me he's out of the country," she whispered back. "We have to try to draw out information from his relatives without letting them know what we're doing."

He cast her a look. "I guess this is where your expertise comes in—drawing out information when the interviewee doesn't want to budge."

"I guess so. If I do have a gift, then I should put it to good use." She grabbed hold of his arm. "Let me do the talking, Jim. Please."

He nodded reluctantly, though his submissiveness did little to calm Leah's apprehension. For an instant she regretted sharing the information, knowing Jim's volatility in light of Kathy's death. Perhaps she would have done better to keep her mouth shut about the whole thing. *It's too late now. I have to keep going, no matter what.*

Leah and Jim slipped in the rear door of the restaurant. The aroma of Mexican food wafted in the air, accompanied by the sound of foreign voices shouting at each other from the kitchen. Leah offered a smile at a waitress who brushed by them, waving her order pad in the air. When the waitress returned, carrying a platter of steaming enchiladas, Leah caught her elbow.

"I spoke with someone here in the restaurant who is the brother of Miguel. Miguel used to teach Spanish at Taylor Elementary School, right?"

"Sí. He no work now. Why?"

The information spawned confidence. "Miguel's brother said he would provide me the information I needed about hiring a Spanish teacher. I talked to him earlier today."

"You talk with Eduardo?" asked the waitress.

"Eduardo? Yes, that's him. We had an appointment. Can you show us to his office, and we'll wait for him there?"

"Pedro!" she yelled, speaking in rapid Spanish while thrusting a plate into the hands of a nearby waiter. She then turned and said in English to Leah and Jim, "Come this way."

Leah followed the petite woman to a small door with Jim close at her heels. "Eduardo be back soon. Wait for him."

"Thank you, we will wait. Would you have any idea why Miguel left? I was going to offer a hundred dollars a lesson if he could teach me Spanish. I heard he was the best."

The waitress blinked. "I don't know why he left. I think he scared."

"Scared?"

The waitress nodded. "Things no go well here. People mad at him. He got scared." She drew closer. "Miguel and I go out, you know. Then he leaves without telling me good-bye."

"Really? That's terrible. The nerve of him."

"He said he would marry me, you know. Then he goes away without a word. He left after that shooting at the school. Eduardo says he was scared. I say, why he scared? Eduardo no tell me. Says it's none of my business." She showed Leah a diamond ring on her finger—larger than anything she had ever seen in her life. "He give me this."

"It's gorgeous! I don't understand why he would leave you."

"I don't, either. But I keep the ring. They say it worth a lo of money. If he leave, then I keep the ring." She tossed he head. "Maybe sell it and get a lot of money for myself."

Leah smiled. "Thank you so much. . ." She glanced at th nametag. "Maria. And I hope you will get over this okay I can't believe this happened to you." The girl offered a fair smile before leaving the room. Leah turned to find the offic filled to capacity with junk. A computer lay buried beneath mound of paper.

"That didn't get us anywhere," Jim said.

"Actually, she did say Miguel was scared. Scared of wha I wonder?" Leah went over to the desk and began shufflin through the paper covering the computer monitor. Beside rested stacks of the *Gainsport Herald*. "These are recen receipts from the restaurant that will probably go into th computer database. Jim, go stand by the door and listen fo anyone heading in this direction. I'm going to see if there' any information tucked inside the computer."

"I doubt you'll find anything."

Leah booted up the machine. "It's worth a try. Lots of busi nesses are keeping records on the computer these days Maybe there will be some clue." She searched the main menu only to find the typical programs available for use. "Nothin much," she sighed, her eyes drifting to a computer disk sittin on the desk with the word *Trabajo* written on it. From he schooling in Spanish, she remembered the word mean "work." Leah immediately inserted the disk and tried to ope the Excel file. The screen asked for a password. She type in Trabajo. *Invalid file name*. "Oh!" She frowned and typed i Miguel. *Invalid file name* again flashed before her eyes.

"Leah, you'll never get that thing shut off in time if someon comes walking down the hall," Jim said. "I don't think th owner will be too happy, finding us playing with his computer."

She ignored his warning and typed Miguel Ramirez. *Invali*

password. She tapped her fingernails on the table. She tried La Casa Restaurante, Colombia, Taylor Elementary, and even Kathy Richards. "What other names are there? What if it's a family name of the Ramirezes? I'll never find anything. Maybe this is the wrong disk anyway."

"Leah. . .give it up."

Her gaze drifted to the stacks of *Gainsport Herald*. On a whim she typed in each word. Under the word *Herald* a spreadsheet materialized before her eyes with dates, numbers, and contacts. The initials COC caught her eye, along with kilograms delivered and monetary amounts in the thousands. "Oh, wow, I've got something! This is it. I know it. This is what we need."

"Leah, someone's coming," Jim whispered hoarsely.

Leah ejected the disk, stuffed the evidence into her pocket, and switched off the computer just as the door opened. A burly man with dark hair entered, clasping a money sack in one hand.

"What are you doing in here?" he barked. "Who let you in this room?"

"Oh, one of your waitresses," Leah said. "Actually, I couldn't meet with you about the tutoring tomorrow so I came tonight."

He banged the sack on the table. "You no be in here! What were you doing?"

Leah smiled, ushering Jim to the door. "Just waiting, of course. Since I was in the neighborhood, I thought I would stop by. I've waited too long as it is. We're already running late for a dinner appointment, so I must get going. I'll call you tomorrow."

Eduardo blinked, staring at them in confusion. Leah grabbed Jim's hand and hurried him down the hall. "That was close," Jim murmured as they raced for their cars. "You took a big chance."

"It's worth it. That disk will help us figure out what's going on." She felt for the evidence in her pocket. "But we've got to hide it until we can scan the information more closely."

"I'll take it with me."

"Promise me you won't look at it until we can do it together?"

"What's to stop us from looking at it now?" he asked. "I have a computer at home. We can go over there and see what this baby has."

"No, you can't keep it in your home, Jim. You and I are both connected now, and if anyone finds out, our homes are the first places they'll look. Find someone to give it to, someone trustworthy who will keep it for us. When I get free, we'll look at it and find out exactly what is happening."

"I don't understand. . . ," he began. "Look, are you giving me the brush-off because I asked if you were a Christian? There are reasons for this and—"

"No. . .well, look I have to get going. I'll call you when I get through." She flung herself into the car and sped off, her mind awhirl. All the data had been stored under the name of *Herald.* Could the *Gainsport Herald* be linked to Ramirez and, ultimately, to Kathy's death? She knew the moment she stepped into the newspaper office that something was wrong with the place. When she thought about it, everyone there acted as though they were concealing something. Both Haley and Chet had been adamant that she drop the school-shooting case.

A sudden thought crossed her mind. "What am I going to do? Chet works for the *Herald.* Does he know what's going on? Is he in on this?"

Leah turned into the apartment complex, scanning quickly for any sign of the silver car he always drove. "He's not here yet. Thank You, God," she whispered, finding the words easier than they were in the past. "God, I know You're with us. Just like Claire said, I know You're working through all this.

You are a God of justice, aren't You? You want to see justice in all this. Please help us get through this. Show us what to do. And. . .and be with Jim. Help him find a safe place for the disk." An aura of peace descended on her when she finished the prayer. She knew God was at the helm of all this, no matter how many twists and turns she found on this road to justice for a dead woman and her grieving husband.

Leah took out the key to her apartment and inserted it into the keyhole when a gloved hand came from behind and clamped down hard on her wrist. She jerked back. Screams filled her throat. She turned to find a dark figure in a black trench coat and ski mask. He tugged on her arm, leading her to a dark area between several tall bushes.

"Give me the disk!"

Leah shook her head, trying to wriggle herself free from his strong grip. The voice sounded strangely familiar, but she couldn't place it. "I–I don't know what you mean."

"Don't play games. Where is the disk?" His dark hand shook her wrist. "Where? If you don't tell me, you'll regret it, I promise you."

Leah shook her head. Her hand turned numb in the assailant's grip. A sudden thought brought a chilling draft of fear sweeping down on her. *Could this man be Kathy's killer? No! Please. . .please, God, don't let him kill me!*

fifteen

Leah batted open her eyes to find the twinkling stars above her. She struggled to sit up, only to find the bushes spinning around her. All at once, she recalled the stranger who met her outside the apartment door and glanced down to find the red imprint of the assailant's visit decorating her wrist. "It wasn't a dream," she whispered. "It actually happened." Her clothing was disheveled, but he had not raped her as far as she could tell. Leah closed her eyes and thanked God for preserving her life. She found her purse nearby, ravaged by the intruder. In the grass were her keys, cell phone, and wallet. She picked them up and managed to make her way to the apartment door. With shaky fingers, she opened the door and slammed it shut, locking everything tight.

Her mind was a jumble of thoughts. "I have to calm down." Instead, tears welled up and ran down her cheeks. Her teeth chattered madly. Only one thing came to her mind at that moment: Jim. She had to get ahold of Jim and tell him what happened. Jim—the very name brought images of him with his arms around her, holding her close. She reached for the cell phone. It rang endlessly until she heard the click of an answering machine. "You have to be there, Jim," she said into the phone. "It's Leah. Please answer. I need you."

His voice came over the line. "Leah? What's the matter? Are you all right?"

"Help me, Jim! He knows—the killer knows. I'm sure of it. I don't know what we're going to do, but we've stumbled onto something big. Too big. Did you hide the disk?"

"I just got rid of it. It's in a safe place. Are you okay?"

She began to shake. "I don't know. Just come get me."

"I'll come right now. Where are you at?"

"My apartment. When you come, bring someone else's car. And wear a disguise. They're all over the place. They've been watching us. He–he came. . .he wanted to know where the disk is. I don't know how he found out, but—"

"Oh, Leah! I'm coming to get you right now. Just hold tight. Keep the door locked and the window blinds shut. I'll knock three times, then follow with another three knocks. Okay? Hang on."

"Jim. . .Jim. . ." Her voice trailed away as the phone went dead. "I thought I had the strength. I thought I could handle the pressure." She fell back limply on the sofa.

Be strong in the Lord and the strength of His might.

The words came in a still, small voice, yet with strength that lifted her above her circumstances. "Yes, I–I can be strong in God. God is very strong. He's stronger than all the evil in this world. I can trust Him to help me. Oh, God, help me, please!"

She thought back to Claire's words and her need for God. At Claire's church, everyone clung to their Bibles as though they were a source of strength. How she needed that strength at this moment! Somewhere in this apartment, she had a little Bible, given to her by her grandmother at the time of her sister's death. Leah righted herself. She needed that Bible more than anything or anyone at the moment. She managed to stumble to the bookshelf. The Bible was still there on the top shelf gathering dust. Just the feel of the rough leather cover beneath her fingertips brought a measure of comfort.

She went back to the sofa and opened the book to a place marked by a fine, red ribbon. Words jumped out at her about Jesus' death on the cross. In her fear, she remembered Granny giving her the book and telling her about Jesus. It all came back to her now. . .how Jesus, an innocent Man, died so she might be saved. Leah pressed the book to her heart and closed her eyes. "Jesus, I need You. I don't understand what it means to be saved. Help me understand. Please help me get through this night. Save Jim and me!"

❧

Jim arrived in the Hansons' old station wagon. Once he had Leah safely inside the car and heading down the road, she was able to relax a bit, resting her head on his shoulder. He gently stroked her soft cheek, whispering prayers. *Lord, I should have stayed with her. I should've never let her go home alone, not with what we discovered. Thank You, God, for protecting her. Thank You for watching over her.* He traced her sleek hair showering over her shoulder, and her eyelids closed over her weary but beautiful dark eyes. She had displayed such strength the last few days, such determination, such vigor. Now she appeared weary, in need of someone to protect her and help her. *She's done so much for me. She's put her life on the line for me. Lord, show me how I can help her in return. Help us with this next step. Protect us, God.*

A half hour later, Leah stirred, rubbed her eyes, and squinted at the dark shadows of lone trees along the road. "Where are we?"

"We're almost there."

"Where?"

"A friend of Claire's who lives out here in the boonies. His name's Rick. She gave him the disk, and he immediately left for his cabin in the mountains. I called to let him know we're coming. He's been analyzing the data and says he's found some pretty intense stuff."

Leah instantly became alert. "Like what?"

"He didn't go into specifics, but it appears the *Gainsport Herald* was a front for a massive cocaine operation out of Colombia. And the Ramirez guy who worked at Taylor

Elementary? He was likely their principal drug smuggler when he wasn't teaching Spanish. I can't imagine a drug smuggler teaching little kids in an elementary school. It's insane."

Leah clutched his arm, sending sudden warmth rushing through him. The car turned onto a lone dirt road. Lights flickered in the distance. "You sure did pick a remote place to hide our evidence," she mused.

"Only the best." The car pulled to a stop before a rustic home fashioned out of logs. Jim turned to see Leah's face shadowed by the darkness. He heard a slight sniff. Instinctively, he reached for her. "Leah, it's okay."

"I'm really scared. I don't know what's going to happen with all this. I–I had to find God tonight, Jim. I had to. I found an old Bible Granny gave to me back when my sister died. It was still marked with the same passages. I didn't know what it meant, about Jesus dying and all, but Granny said that Jesus died so I can be saved. Does that mean saved from all this?"

"Well, not just from trouble. It's a sense that we need Him to take control of our lives because we're empty without Him. When we surrender to Him, then He fills us with His presence. He saves us from sin and from ourselves. We become a brand-new person on the inside."

"I–I think I felt His presence tonight. I want Him to save me from myself. I don't like what I've done in the past. I want to be a new person. Can I ask Him right now?"

Jim nodded, too overcome at that moment to speak. He prayed silently along with Leah. When she opened her eyes, she appeared even more beautiful to him than before. There were so many words he wanted to say, but they remained choked up within. Not since Kathy had he felt this way about anyone. Leah had ignited something within him. She had relieved him from the burden of despair he thought he would carry the rest of his life.

Now, all the emotion building up within him came forth. He gathered her in his arms. "Leah," he murmured, nuzzling his nose in her hair before seeking out her lips. She relaxed in his arms, her head tilted back, her lips responding to his. The kiss lingered for several wonderful moments.

When she pulled away, a deep breath fanned his face. "Jim, I know I don't understand everything, but am I a Christian?"

"Yes." He hugged her close. "As a famous preacher once said, 'From the top of your head to your pretty little feet, you're covered by Jesus' blood.' "

She smiled. "I'm glad. . .not just because of us. I'm glad because I know we're going to need God more than ever."

❧

Jim and Leah knocked on the door of the cabin. A young man with reddish brown hair and a beard, clad in jeans and a flannel shirt, greeted them. To Leah it seemed hard to believe this man named Rick Malone was Claire's friend.

"So this is the famous private investigator," Rick exclaimed with a grin, shaking Leah's hand. "Claire gave me what you found during the little escapade in the restaurant. I'm pretty impressed. You're one tough lady."

"Not really," Leah said shakily, her fingers intertwined with Jim's. "I just make a show of it."

"There's a song about that—'The Warrior Is a Child.' We look tough on the outside, but on the inside we're kids who need God in a big way, especially when the going gets rough."

"I learned about that," Leah admitted. "I thought I could be a tough lady. . .but found out I couldn't. Claire once told me about trusting in God for everything, even the small things."

Rick's eyes shone at the mention of Claire. "There's no one better to speak with about living for God than Claire." He led the way to the living area. On the table sat a laptop computer, the glowing screen displaying the spreadsheet Leah had discovered at the restaurant.

"It's a huge drug operation, isn't it?" Leah said.

"Yep. Looks like you guys hit the jackpot. Sit down and I'll show you what I've found." With a pencil, he pointed out the tracking of shipments in and out of Colombia, the cash paid, and the deliveries made on behalf of the *Gainsport Herald* newspaper. "Looks like your Ramirez guy was one busy trafficker. I don't know how he had time to teach kids Spanish."

"Do you think he was the target of the shooting?" asked Jim.

Rick nodded. "It makes sense. You hear about these things all the time. A drug operation gone sour. Someone is always trying to knock off another. The day your wife was killed, Jim, the gunman had his eye and his weapon trained on Ramirez. Sad to say, but she got in the way of the bullet."

Jim shook his head. "I don't believe it. Kathy died instead of a drug smuggler. Can you figure out why they wanted him dead?"

"I can't tell from these records. Perhaps he didn't get a shipment to them on time."

"Maybe Ramirez was going to rat to the authorities," suggested Leah. "Or he may have been set to flee that evening."

"I still don't understand why they chose a playground filled with kids," Jim grumbled. "If they want to kill someone, they should do it in a back alley."

"I've said all along that it was a safe front for them, as terrible as it seems," Leah explained. "With all the school shootings, maybe the guy thought it was a good opportunity—kill the man there and make it look like another rampage at a school by some insane kid."

Rick nodded. "Could be. Only the crazy killer knows why he did it there."

He continued to scan the data. "They were making a heap of money in this venture, at any rate. If something went wrong, it's likely someone might have been hired to do away with Ramirez. Hard to believe a small country newspaper like the *Herald* was in on this whole scheme."

"You were suspicious of that newspaper anyway," Jim reminded Leah. "You couldn't stand the editor. And you said Chet Frazier was in on it too. No wonder Frazier wanted the scoop. He was looking to cover himself in all this. He may have even been the one who pulled the trigger."

His observation sent Leah gasping for air. "You mean Chet may have fired the shot that killed Kathy?"

"I wouldn't put it past him. Likely it was someone connected with the paper. Frazier was willing to do anything for his own advancement. No wonder I disliked him from the beginning."

Leah grabbed for a chair to steady herself. The reality of the claim made her dizzy. Just the notion she might have eaten with a killer and even kissed him sent her thoughts into disarray. She trembled and folded her arms to control her jitters, but her teeth continued to chatter. Jim wrapped a warm arm around her to calm the tremors. "This is way too big, Jim," she murmured. "I don't know what to think. Just the idea that all this was happening at the *Gainsport Herald*—the very place where I work. I–I feel like I'm involved or responsible, having been associated with Chet and the *Herald*. I don't know what to do."

Jim took her hand in his and squeezed it. "Leah, you had no idea what was going on. Those crooks hid their deeds well. You were able to find out the truth. You've done a great job." He whispered the thought in such a way that sparked a tingly sensation within her. When she turned her head, his lips paid a gentle call on her own. "Leah, I owe everything to you. I mean it. Without you, I—"

At that moment, the sound of car engines and tires crunching the gravel of the driveway announced some unexpected visitors. Rick peeked through the blinds. In an instant, he ejected the disk from the laptop and handed it and an extra copy he'd made to Jim. "We've got visitors. Jim, get out of here now! Take the disks with you."

Jim took the disks from his outstretched hand. "What about you, Rick?"

Something slammed into the door, rattling it on its hinges.

"I'll try to hold them off and call 911. There's a small trap door in the floor under the desk that leads to the cellar. When you get there, climb out the small door to your right and head for the woods."

Jim grabbed Leah's hand. "C'mon," he said, dragging her by the arm. He crawled beneath the desk to find the small door built into the floorboards. "C'mon, Leah," he whispered as shouts came from outside the cabin, along with the shatter of glass.

"Jim. . .what if they hurt Rick?" Leah whispered, groping her way down a few steps into the dankness of a small storage room until they found a little door set high in the wall.

"We've got to trust God, Leah." He fumbled in the darkness to open the latch. "C'mon, climb up on my shoulders. We need to go through here. It must lead outside."

She did so, shaking like a leaf, her hair blowing in the wind as she climbed out of the door and fell to the ground. Jim was right behind her. They hastened for the woods just as the men entered the cabin. A shot rang out.

"Jim!" Leah cried, panting from the run. "They shot Rick! What are we going to do?"

"Leah, we can't let them get ahold of these disks. Just run."

Behind them came the banter of voices and the snapping of saplings, announcing the pursuers.

"What are we going to do?" Leah cried.

"Just keep going. We have to keep going. We can't stop."

Branches snagged her clothing and stung as they slapped her. Twigs poked into her legs. *Don't stop*, her mind urged. *Keep going. Don't hesitate and don't look back*. Thoughts of the killer and his cohorts in hot pursuit forced her onward, even as her muscles began to go into spasms and her breathing became erratic.

After twenty minutes of struggling through the thick underbrush, Jim found a rocky hillside and a small cave where they crawled inside. Sounds of labored breathing filled the cavern's interior. They huddled together in the darkness, waiting and listening for any signs of their pursuers. The silence made them rest a bit easier.

Leah rubbed her cramped leg muscles, all the while trying to control the fear welling up within her. "I never thought it might come to this. I should have known it would, but all I wanted to do was find the answers."

"And we have the answer, thanks to you." Jim pulled the disks from his pocket. "This is all the evidence the police need to put away those who murdered Kathy." He studied the wall of the cave until he found some loose rocks. He yanked out several chunks of limestone, shoved the disks into two separate spaces, and covered the holes.

"Why are you doing that?"

"Just in case. We can always come back for them when the danger has passed."

Leah clung to his arm. "Y–You don't think the danger is over?"

Jim shook his head before closing his eyes, reflecting over the events of that night. "It isn't over until the police catch them. God, please watch over Rick. Please help him."

"Yes, God." Leah joined him. "Please keep him and us safe."

"Rick was a good friend of Claire's," Jim murmured. "I used to kid her about him. I thought they would make a great couple." He shook his head before falling silent.

Leah pressed her face into his shirt, inhaling the rugged scent of the outdoors, thankful that he was there by her side.

She didn't want to ponder what might have happened to the man who helped them analyze the disk, fearing he had met the same fate as Kathy Richards. They sat hidden there for an hour, listening and waiting, hoping for a chance to return to the cabin and check on Rick.

After a time, Jim released his hold on Leah. "I'll check if they're gone. We've got to get back to the cabin if possible and help Rick."

Leah nodded, watching Jim slowly inch his way out of the cave. He appeared tall and commanding in the shadows of the night. He descended the hill and went through the woods. She huddled her arms close to protect herself from the chill of the cave, praying the men had given up the chase. The solitude of the surrounding forest, serenaded only by the chatter of insects, fueled her confidence.

At the sound of crashing limbs and voices, she jumped to her feet. Her heart nearly ceased to beat. "Jim!" She crawled out of the cave to find Jim being dragged up the hill by two men. Her eyes widened in horror. One of the men was Sam Warner, the would-be custodian who worked at the *Gazette*. In his hand he brandished a pistol. The other was a tall man with dark hair. *Chet.* Leah nearly fainted. The nightmare had come true.

"So it's the dynamic duo, out to catch the bad guys," Chet said with a scornful chuckle. "Dear Leah, how many times did I warn you to stay out of all this? Why didn't you listen to me?"

Leah watched Sam jerk Jim's arm up behind his back. Jim winced in pain.

"Stop it! Let him go."

"Of course. Hand over the disk, and we'll be on our way."

Leah could see Jim's eyes searching hers. The look in them pleaded with her not to give in. "I–I don't have it."

Chet strode up to her and glared. "You try my patience." He gripped her wrist. "Where's the disk."

The fateful words spoken earlier that evening came back to haunt her. *Chet was the one who grabbed me by the door! He was the man dressed in black!* "I–I don't have it," she repeated.

Chet whirled to face Jim. "All right then. Richards, where's the disk?"

Jim said nothing. Sam again wrenched his arm. "You'd better tell him," Sam muttered.

"We don't have it," Jim retorted. "It. . .we dropped it in the woods. Sorry."

"You dropped it," Chet repeated. "How clumsy of you."

"Let's bump them off," Sam said. "They're no help to us, anyway. They know too much."

Chet turned, surveying Leah, who retreated when Sam raised his gun. "No."

"But we have to," Sam protested. "We don't have a choice."

Chet shook his head. "Frank didn't give the order. And we don't have the disk."

"I don't care. They both know. You can't let them go. It's me that will get fried in all this anyway. I'm the one who'll get in trouble. It's my gut on the line. You kept your hands clean while I did all the dirty work. Now you're gonna let them go, so I'm the one who ends up in the slammer?"

"Shut up," Chet snapped at Sam.

Leah stared at the custodian who had trailed her while she worked for the *Bakersville Gazette*. "It was you! You did it. How could you do something like that—kill an innocent teacher in front of her students? How could you fire into a playground? Are you insane?"

"I wasn't trying to kill her," Sam said, his voice wavering. "It was an accident. Honest. I was trying to—"

"Will you shut up!" Chet snarled at Sam. "You don't know when to keep quiet, do you? You gotta go and flap that mouth of yours!"

With the men preoccupied, Jim wrestled his way out of Sam's hold. A blow from his fist sent Sam sailing to the ground where his head plowed into a thick tree trunk. The gun fell out of his hand. Before Jim could reach it, Chet swiped it up and trained it on him.

"Stay right there, Richards," he said in a guarded voice. "That's it. Now I'll give you five seconds to tell me where that disk is before you join your wife in the happy hunting ground in the sky."

"Chet, please don't," Leah begged.

"What do you see in him anyway, Leah? I love you with everything in me. I love your spirit, your life, your beauty. I'd give you anything you want."

"There's nothing you have that I want," Leah hissed. "You were deceptive from the beginning, leading me on like you were some hotshot reporter when you knew what had happened that day at Taylor Elementary." Her gaze dropped to Sam, who still lay on the ground at the foot of the tree.

"You've forgotten one thing. There is something I have that you want: Jim Richards." His finger tightened over the trigger. "I have his life in my hand. Don't you see?"

"Chet, please."

"Now tell me about the disk you stole from the restaurant. You know where it is, don't you? You wouldn't have been so careless and dropped it. You've been thorough from the beginning. Your only mistake was telling me your plans. I guess we did have a little matter of trust between us, didn't we?" His hand began to shake. "Now where's the disk? Tell me where that disk is or so help me. . ." The gun fired, sending a bullet whizzing past Jim and into a tree.

"In the cave," she said quickly. "Please don't hurt Jim."

"Thank you. That's better. Now go and get it."

"Chet, please don't do this," Leah said in a soft voice. "This is wrong. You know it's wrong. Give this up."

Chet swallowed hard and stammered, "I–I can't."

"Yes, you can."

"I'm in too far, Leah. You don't know Frank. If I don't get my hands on that disk. . ." He shuddered. "I–I'm a dead man. He's got his own people, you know. I'm in too far."

She stepped toward him, ignoring the gun he held, to help a man caught in the throes of a diabolical web that entangled his soul. "Then live, Chet. I know you want to live. You love life. You can't kill."

"You underestimate me. I will kill if it saves my neck. And I need that disk. So get it now. I mean it." The gun began to shake.

Leah crawled into the cave and retrieved a disk from the small niche that Jim had created in the rocky wall. She came out and flung the disk at Chet. "Here's your disk." Chet stuffed the disk into the pocket of his jacket. "I'm sorry to say this, but Sam was right." He lifted the gun. "I can't just leave you two here to rat on me, can I?"

Leah inhaled sharply. "Chet, you can't do this. You're not that kind of person. Sam maybe. . .but he's not like you. I know you. I know you could have taken advantage of me . . .of our relationship. I've seen how many times you tried to protect me, to keep me from getting hurt, even though I was investigating the very thing you were involved in."

The gun wavered in his hand. "Leah, you don't realize how much I love you. It was a mistake to fall in love with you. Frank told me to forget you, to let you go before it was too late. I couldn't. I tried to get you to stop with the investigation. You kept pressing, wanting to find out who killed Kathy Richards. I knew once you did, it would be the end for us."

"Chet, you know it's the end," she said, watching out of the corner of her eye as Jim stealthily approached Chet from the side.

"I don't want it to be the end. I don't, Leah."

With a quick maneuver, Jim delivered a blow to Chet's right arm, dislodging the gun. Leah quickly picked it up, even as Chet stared at her, clutching his injured forearm, his face contorted in pain like a wounded animal. All at once, the woods were filled with police who came with dogs barking and flashlights illuminating the darkness. Jim and Leah held each other, breathing prayers of relief as the authorities handcuffed both Chet and Sam and led them away.

sixteen

"Claire, how did you ever think to come here?" Jim marveled, watching the ambulance and police cars that now surrounded the small cabin deep within the woods.

His sister hugged him close. "Before you came to see Rick, he called and told me what happened. I knew eventually the police would have to be in on this." Tears trickled out of her eyes as Rick was rolled out on a stretcher. She rushed forward, her hand reaching out to him.

"I–I'm okay," Rick murmured, managing a faint smile. "I ducked in time. I only got hit in the shoulder."

"Is he really okay?" she asked the paramedic who held up a bag of intravenous fluid with a tube running into Rick's arm.

"He may need surgery to remove the bullet," the paramedic said. "He's one lucky guy."

"Oh, Rick. God watched over you."

"He sure did. I–I'm glad you got the police, Claire."

Claire nodded, even as Leah ventured forward to console her. "He's going to be fine, Claire. He was very brave tonight. . . buying us the time we needed."

Claire turned and embraced Leah like a sister would, sharing her tears. "I shouldn't be the one crying like this," Claire sniffed. "You were both the ones who went through it all."

"Everything came out all right in the end," Leah said soothingly, even as several detectives ventured forward to obtain statements from Jim and her. Others analyzed the crime scene within the cabin. Leah shivered, reminding herself that this was not another murder, but the resolution of a year-long nightmare. When she turned to Jim, he stood silently in the background with his hands deep in his pockets, surveying the flash of lights illuminating the cabin in brilliant light. Leah approached him, fearful over what might be radiating through his mind.

"Are you okay, Jim?"

He shrugged. "I guess. After all this time, I thought I would feel a great relief that the killer had been nabbed. Yet I still feel empty. The whole thing was meaningless. Kathy died for a cocaine ring." He kicked up a mound of dirt. "There is no satisfaction in learning the truth, Leah."

Leah stood by silently, even as the police car drove away, bearing the guilty party. She took up his hand. "Remember me telling you about that old Bible Granny gave to me when Sophie died? She told me about Jesus and how these bad men had put Him to death, even though He was innocent. I didn't want to believe it. I was so upset at the time, I thought God didn't care. But after reading over those passages and realizing what happened to Jesus, Granny's words made sense. Jesus' death on the cross brings the peace and the justice we need, because He went through it. He understands. He knows."

Jim remained silent.

"I know this is hard, but without this whole thing, I might not have had a reason to search for God. I wouldn't have remembered Granny's words either." Leah wiped a tear from her eye. "It gives meaning to those we lost. Their deaths really brought forth life—a new person like me. . .a new Christian. Let's not think about death anymore, Jim. Let's think about life."

❧

Leah found herself overwhelmed by reporters and detectives wishing to interview her. After being hounded by reporters seeking news, she understood all too well Jim's reaction to reporters in the aftermath of Kathy's death. The evening news replayed the scenes of detectives swarming the newspaper office of the *Gainsport Herald* where she once worked. The familiar sight of the offices and hallway sent shivers racing through her.

"Frank Haley and several employees of the *Gainsport Herald* were taken into custody today after the discovery of their involvement in the drug smuggling ring. The shot which accidentally killed the third-grade teacher at Taylor Elementary last year was intended to hit one of their drug runners."

Leah set down the mug of tea. She glanced over at the phone, wishing with all her heart that she could talk to Jim. No doubt he now found himself inundated once again with media attention. She had heard little from him. Calls to his home went unanswered. After several days passed, Leah finally went over and picked up the phone. It rang ten times before she gave up. "Jim probably assumes I'm a reporter." The notion made her think about the old days.

She jumped into the car and headed for Markman's Nursery. The same lady who had sold her the impatiens that decorated Jim's front yard greeted her.

"I'd like a rosebush, please," Leah said.

"What kind are you looking for? We have many varieties. Queen Elizabeth, Purple Passion, Red Blaze—that's a climbing rose—John F. Kennedy. . ."

"I'd like a red variety."

"Mr. Lincoln is an excellent red rose." The saleslady showed her a bush with red buds ready to burst forth in vivid color.

"That looks fine." Leah paid for the rosebush and carried it to her car, careful to avoid the prickly thorns. When she arrived at Jim's house, she saw him with a hose in his hand, carefully watering the row of impatiens that had produced a glorious display of color since the day she planted them.

Leah bit her lip. Would he even want to see her after all that had happened? It had been a week since the escapade at Rick's cabin, yet despite the terror of it all, she felt a bond with Jim. Looking at the rosebush on the floor of the car, she compared the beauty of it to life itself. Like the beauty of the rose that overshadows the thorns, so too, God's love overcomes the pains of life. Leah lifted the large bush out of the car and walked toward him.

"Jim."

He turned with the hose and accidentally sprayed her sneakers. "Oops!" He rushed for the faucet. "Sorry, Leah. I was just going to call you when I got done here. I know I haven't been in touch."

"That's okay. I brought you a present." Leah placed the bush on the ground. "I thought this symbolized what we've both been through."

Jim stared. "A rosebush?"

"A Mr. Lincoln, to be exact. The saleslady at the nursery said the bush would put out the most beautiful red roses. The directions for planting are on the tag."

"A good thing. I've never planted one, despite all the gardening I've done." He gazed at her. "I hope you're not mad I haven't called. I've been staying at Claire's. She's been running back and forth to the hospital. I think she needed the support, with Rick being hurt. She was there for me. I owed her big time. Rick got out of the hospital yesterday, so I came home."

"How is he?"

"Doing well. The bullet narrowly missed a major artery. It took some doing to get the bullet out. He's been on antibiotic treatment for a good part of the week, but he told Claire he would have given up both arms to see justice carried out."

"I was glad for his help." Leah closed her eyes for a moment, thankful it was all over but for the memories.

Suddenly, she felt a tender hand wipe a stray tear from her cheek.

"I'm so glad God brought you into my life," Jim murmured. "If it weren't for you, Leah. . .I'd be hopeless, helpless, a regular basket case. I know I said that Kathy's death was meaningless. . . ."

"Jim, it wasn't meaningless. It may have looked that way at first, but God made something good come out of it. Look at how many people were saved because of Kathy. Not only did she help save students' lives, but her death also helped to bust open a huge cocaine ring that could have hurt so many people. And if it weren't for you and Claire, I'd be a nosy reporter without God, probably making people and myself miserable."

Jim stared at her, unblinking, before gathering her in his arms. "Leah, what would I do without you? God used you too. You brought meaning back into my life when I thought I would never have any again."

Both of them drew together for a kiss. Suddenly, Jim pulled away. A sheepish grin spread across his face. He lifted his hand and waved.

"Jim, what are you doing?" Leah turned to see Emma Hanson standing in the living-room window of her house, waving. A window slowly came up.

"I just knew it!" she exclaimed in glee through the screen. "You two were meant to be."

Jim and Leah turned to embrace each other. They couldn't help but agree.

A Letter To Our Readers

Dear Reader:

In order that we might better contribute to your reading enjoyment, we would appreciate your taking a few minutes to respond to the following questions. We welcome your comments and read each form and letter we receive. When completed, please return to the following:

Rebecca Germany, Fiction Editor
Heartsong Presents
PO Box 719
Uhrichsville, Ohio 44683

1. Did you enjoy reading *A Rose Among Thorns* by Lauralee Bliss?

   ❑ Very much! I would like to see more books by this author!

   ❑ Moderately. I would have enjoyed it more if

   ____

   ____

2. Are you a member of **Heartsong Presents**? Yes ❑ No ❑
   If no, where did you purchase this book?______________

   ____

3. How would you rate, on a scale from 1 (poor) to 5 (superior), the cover design?______________________________

4. On a scale from 1 (poor) to 10 (superior), please rate the following elements.

   _____ Heroine _____ Plot

   _____ Hero _____ Inspirational theme

   _____ Setting _____ Secondary characters

5. These characters were special because________________

____

____

6. How has this book inspired your life?________________

____

____

7. What settings would you like to see covered in future **Heartsong Presents** books?________________

____

____

8. What are some inspirational themes you would like to see treated in future books?________________

____

____

9. Would you be interested in reading other **Heartsong Presents** titles? Yes ❑ No ❑

10. Please check your age range:

❑ Under 18 ❑ 18-24 ❑ 25-34

❑ 35-45 ❑ 46-55 ❑ Over 55

Name ____

Occupation ___________________________________

Address ______________________________________

City ________________ State __________ Zip __________

Email ____